MONK'S HOLLOW

An assorted company of young people come to Monk's Hollow, summoned there by a mysterious letter from Agatha Pentland, a rich old recluse, who intends to make one of them her heir. Amongst the guests are the son of an old friend, the daughter of her dead husband's business partner, and a young TV actor whose father loved Agatha Pentland many years ago, all strangers to Mrs Pentland. The visitors soon suspect that the house is haunted by a malevolent spirit which threatens not only Mrs Pentland's life, but their own safety as well.

MONK'S HOLLOW

by
John Marsh

Published in Large Print ... by arrangement with John Long/Hale.

Dales Large Print Books
Long Preston, North Yorkshire,
England.

British Library Cataloguing in Publication Data.

Marsh, John
   Monk's Hollow.

A catalogue record for this book is
available from the British Library

ISBN 1-85389-782-5 pbk

First published in Great Britain by John Gifford Ltd., 1968

Dales Large Print is an imprint of
Library Magna Books Ltd.
Printed and bound in Great Britain by
T.J. International Ltd., Cornwall, PL28 8RW.

Contents

Contents

1

A Cold Journey

Sally Morgan peered anxiously through the window at the driving snow which hid the dark countryside.

She felt very cold and not a little scared.

The train was late. Suppose the connection for Darkling Halt had left! What would she do then marooned at a small country junction, probably miles from anywhere, on Christmas Eve?

She was alone. Though several people had entered the compartment at Liverpool Street two hours before, they had, one by one, disappeared into the snowy darkness at one or other of the small stations at which the train had stopped.

To fill the time Sally opened her handbag and took out the letter she had received a few days before.

The writing was spidery and shaky but she had no difficulty in reading it in the light of the single low power bulb which was all British Rail had provided to dispel the darkness of an early winter's evening.

'My Dear Niece,' she read, 'I would like you to spend Christmas with me at Monk's Hollow and will expect you to arrive on Christmas Eve. You will take a train from Liverpool Street to Bleakley Junction, there changing for Darkling Halt, the nearest station to Monk's Hollow. I enclose five pounds to cover your expenses. Yours, Agatha Pentland.'

As she replaced the letter in its envelope Sally recalled her anger when she had first read it. How dare this old woman, who had chosen to ignore her existence for twenty years, summon her to her side in such a peremptory manner? Why, for all Agatha Pentland knew, she might have made other plans.

Everybody else at the office had gone home for Christmas, for instance. Why then should her great-aunt, who knew nothing about her, have assumed that she would be staying over the festive season in her lonely digs?

And to send that five pounds! Almost as if she was a servant being sent her fare to go to a new job.

Yet as the days passed and Christmas drew nearer, Sally's indignation lessened. Hearing the other girls at the office talking excitedly of the Christmas that lay ahead of them, and knowing that her own would be spent shut away in the lonely little room where she had lived since her father died two years before, she had begun to think more charitably of the old lady and her unexpected invitation.

Her mind had finally been made up for her by her landlady who told her, on the day before Christmas Eve, that she and her husband were going to spend Christmas Day with friends and that they were afraid they'd have to leave Sally alone in the house.

Up to that point Sally had clung to the thought that she would at least be able to have Christmas dinner with kindly Mrs Best and her husband, as she had done the year before. Now even that little treat was to be denied her.

When Mrs Best had apologised Sally had said impulsively:

'As a matter of fact I'm going away

myself. I've just had an invitation from an old aunt to stay with her over Christmas.'

She didn't add that she'd never even set eyes on Aunt Agatha, that always the old woman—who lived in the depths of Suffolk—had ignored her, even after her father died.

Sally, staring out into the snowy darkness, thought of her father's angry face as he had told her about his aunt, and how, after bringing him up after his parents were killed in a car smash, she had put him out of her life after he had married a girl whom she had considered far beneath her in the social scale.

The fact that Sally's mother had died after five years of perfect happiness, had intensified rather than lessened Henry Morgan's bitterness against the old woman. He had made no effort to get in touch with her, and she, for her part, had not written to him, though there had been no reason why she should as he had not told her of his wife's death.

She had been told, of course, when Sally's father had died. Mr Thompson, the solicitor, who had settled Henry Morgan's small affairs, had written to the old lady, though there had been no reply.

Mr Thompson had been shocked.

'To leave you to fend for yourself at your age!' he had cried.

Sally had laughed. 'I'm eighteen and quite old enough to earn my own living, Mr Thompson,' she had said more bravely than she felt. 'Don't worry about me. I've got the little bit of money Daddy left as a nest egg, and I've got a good job. I'll be all right.'

But it had been a hard struggle in the last two years and Sally had only just managed to keep her head above water.

Sometimes alone in her little room she had felt frightened wondering what life held for her. She knew hardly anyone but the girls at the office and most of her free time was spent walking in the parks, visiting a cinema or sitting alone in her bed-sitting-room.

Often she cried herself to sleep longing for the companionship of the father whom she had loved so very deeply.

The train, coming to an abrupt halt then moving forward again in a number of jerks and jolts, roused Sally from her reverie.

Looking out she saw lights glimmering alongside and realised that the first part of the journey was over. She dragged down

11

her suitcase from the rack, opened the door of the compartment and stepped down on to the snow-covered platform.

No one else, so far as she could see, had alighted with her from the London train. She began to walk towards the barrier thinking that a ticket collector would tell her what she wanted to know. The suitcase, though not very heavy, was awkward to carry along the slippery platform. Sally, afraid of missing her connection, quickened her pace. It was an unwise thing to do, as she realised feeling her feet slipping away under her. She would have fallen heavily but at that moment a strong hand closed over her elbow and steadied her. She turned and found herself looking into a lean tanned face under the brim of a rather large felt hat. The man's white teeth gleamed in a cheerful grin as he met her eyes.

'Steady! This platform's like a skating rink.'

His deep pleasant voice had a suspicion of a drawl. Was he an American or an Australian? Sally wondered.

'I was trying to find someone who could tell me where I could get the train to Darkling Halt,' she said a little breathlessly. 'I think it leaves in a few minutes.'

He was dressed in a thick belted overcoat and carried a bulky grip. Releasing her arm he took her suitcase from her as if it was the most natural thing in the world.

'I'm going to Darkling Halt as well,' he said. 'We go over the bridge to the platform at the far side.'

She walked along by his side stealing an occasional glance at his big broad-shouldered form and rather homely features. She wondered why he was going to Darkling Halt. Surely he couldn't also be visiting Aunt Agatha!

'I gather there's only one house of any consequence near Darkling Halt,' he said, as if in answer to her unspoken question. 'I'm a guest at Monk's Hollow for Christmas. It would be nice to think that you were too, Miss—Miss—'

Sally smiled. 'The name's Sally Morgan. And—yes! I am going to stay at Monk's Hollow. It's my Aunt Agatha's house.'

He looked at her with frank curiosity. 'Now this is really interesting! You must be Agatha Pentland's nephew's child. I've heard my mother speak often of your father and how tragic it was that Mrs Pentland didn't see eye to eye with him in his choice of a wife.'

They had reached the other side of the bridge now. In a siding stood a small, rather battered looking train of three coaches, with an ancient engine waiting to take it on its way through the gathering darkness.

The young man—Sally decided he was about twenty-five—opened the door of a compartment and put the two bags on the rack before helping Sally in. There was no heating and Sally, sitting in a corner facing her companion, buried her cold hands in her coat pockets. A tiny gas jet, enclosed in a dirty white bowl fastened to the roof, shed a flickering yellow light which did little to dispel the gloom.

'My mother was Agatha Pentland's best friend at one time,' the young man went on. 'When she married my father and went to live in New Zealand she kept up a correspondence over the years. Once or twice she has come to England on holiday and has always come to stay at Monk's Hollow with her friend Agatha. Now—well, she died last year after a severe illness.'

Sally's pretty face softened in sympathy.

'I'm so sorry,' she murmured. He smiled sadly. 'It was a big blow at the time, but I'm gradually getting over it. My father is running the farm and he persuaded me to come to England for a holiday. When I arrived a week ago I wrote to Mrs Pentland and said I would like to come and see her. She replied immediately, asking me for Christmas, which is why I'm here now.'

With a shuddering jolt the little train drew itself together and began to move out of the station. Sally, looking across at the young man, realised how she had seemed to take him on trust from the very first moment she met him. Ordinarily she would have thought twice before she had entered an old-fashioned compartment like this with a complete stranger for a journey which might last for half an hour or more.

'By the way, I haven't told you my name yet,' the young man said. 'For the record it's Alec Carpenter.'

'Did your mother tell you anything more about my father except that Aunt Agatha had refused to have anything to do with him after he married my mother?' Sally asked as the train chugged its way through the snowy countryside.

'At the time my mother received the letters I don't think I took much notice of the extracts she read from them to my father,' Alec Carpenter said. 'But after she died I found all her letters and read them through. You were mentioned quite a lot. Apparently Mrs Pentland, though she hadn't kept in touch with your father over the years, knew all about him, and about you too. I should say she had regular reports sent to her.'

Sally's eyes flashed indignantly. 'Do you mean she had someone spying on us?'

He laughed. 'I don't think she went so far as that. I should imagine she would get her solicitor to check up on you occasionally to see if you had moved your address or anything. That's all.'

'That explains how she knew where to write to me about coming to her for Christmas,' Sally said. 'She sounds a most peculiar person, I must say.'

For a moment he frowned. 'I wouldn't call her peculiar. My mother thought the world of her. I imagine, from what I've heard, that your father and your aunt were of a similar character, both as stubborn as mules. Having had this terrible quarrel after your father married your mother neither would admit to being wrong, and as no overtures were made the situation just dragged on and on.'

'But you would have thought she would have got in touch with me when my father died,' Sally murmured. 'The solicitor wrote and told her.'

'Did you stay at the same address after your father died?' Alec asked.

She shook her head. 'No, for one thing the flat where we lived was too expensive for me to keep up and for another I couldn't bear to go on living in a place where I'd been so happy with my father. I packed up and disappeared. I got another job about that time and went into digs.'

'Doesn't it occur to you that your aunt might have lost touch with you then?' the man asked. 'It may only have been recently that she caught up with you again.'

Sally saw the reasonableness of this but she did not say anything, only stared out of the dirty window at the whirling snow and the darkness outside. She rather resented this young man sticking up for Aunt Agatha. After all, the old woman had had no right to try to influence her father as to whom he should marry. That was his business. And she must have seen how terribly happy he was in the few years he and her mother had been together.

Ten minutes later the little train came to a shuddering halt alongside a platform deep in snow. A single lamp attached to a high wooden fence lit up the name board with its legend—'Darkling Halt'.

'Here we are!' Alec Carpenter cried, jumping to his feet and reaching up for Sally's suitcase and his grip. 'Be careful as you get out. That platform looks very treacherous.'

A young porter, his cap pushed to the back of his curly head, his shoulders white with snow, walked down the train looking for alighting passengers. He seized the handle, opened the door so that Sally could jump down. Alec followed with the luggage.

'Can we get a taxi to take us out to Monk's Hollow?' the young New Zealander asked.

'Be you guests for Mrs Pentland's?' the porter asked, and when Sally nodded, 'There be a car outside now waiting for ye. I'll take your tickets, thank'ee.'

They made for the barrier and saw an old saloon car waiting in the road outside. A middle-aged man, huddled in

18

a thick overcoat, leaned out of the window and asked them if they were for Monk's Hollow. Alec nodded and opened the back door for Sally to climb into the dark interior and sink on the well worn cushions.

The old car, windscreen wipers scrabbling frantically at the settling snow, moved cautiously off along the narrow road. The rather feeble headlights lit up the high hedges on either side, which seemed likely to collapse at any moment under their burden of snow.

'How far is Monk's Hollow, driver?' Alec asked the huddled figure at the wheel.

'Just over half a mile,' came back the muffled reply. 'I doubt if I'll be able to get up the drive to the house. I don't mind telling you if it hadn't been for Mrs Pentland I'd never have turned out tonight. Madness, that's what it is!'

Sally suddenly felt herself possessed of a powerful desire to giggle. Alec, leaning forward a little said: 'You're the local taxi, are you?'

'That's right. Mrs Pentland's one of my best customers. I wouldn't have turned out for anybody else.'

No more was said until after skidding

round numerous bends and turns the car drew up outside a pair of tall iron gates. The driver glanced round.

'This is as far as I can take you,' he said. 'It's not far to the house up the drive.'

'But I can't see that the drive will be any worse than this road,' Alec protested. 'It's too bad expecting us to walk through the snow with our bags—'

'I'm sorry, sir,' the man said firmly. 'If I tried to set off up that steep drive I'd never get more than half-way. I'd probably find myself there for the night.'

Alec helped Sally out into the snow and lifted out the two bags.

'How much do I owe you?' he asked the driver, but the man muttering something about Mrs Pentland paying, let in the clutch and sent the old car skidding off into the darkness.

2

Monk's Hollow

A biting wind now whirled the snow into the faces of the two young people as they breasted the steep drive which ran through what appeared to be a wood. It was very dark but the resourceful Alec had produced a small torch when they left the road and this helped them find their way up the slope.

Sally was glad that she had decided to start out on her journey wearing rubber ankle boots. The conditions underfoot would have completely ruined a lighter pair of shoes by this time.

'I wonder how far it is,' she said after a few minutes, stopping in the middle of the drive to get her breath.

'I'm sure it can't be far now,' the young man encouraged. 'I think I saw a gleam of light through the trees a few minutes ago.'

They went on again and, reaching the

top of the steep rise, they came out of the trees to find the dark bulk of a house facing them a couple of hundred yards away. Lights gleamed in several windows. Sally and Alec paused to look at it.

'It's very big,' Sally said.

Alec nodded. 'It reminds me of a Christmas card I once had as a boy. At that time I'd never seen any snow. This old house, with lights shining from its windows, and the snow whirling outside, seems to me like something out of fairyland.'

Sally, looking at the house's pointed gables and tall chimneys, shivered suddenly. 'It looks the sort of house you expect to see a witch on a broomstick riding over,' she said with a shaky little laugh.

Alec Carpenter grinned down at her.

'Oh, I'm sure it's not as bad as that, Sally!' he cried. 'I'll admit it does look a bit isolated, but I dare say when the sun's shining it will look cheerful enough.'

The drive, which had climbed through the trees, now went sharply down a slope to the house which stood in a hollow surrounded by parkland. Snow-covered lawns came almost up to the walls of the house. There was an open space bounded by a stone balustrade in front of the porticoed entrance.

Alec and Sally trudged through the snow to this door and Alec, after looking in vain for a bell, rapped on it with an old-fashioned knocker. There was a pause, then slowly the door was opened.

A white-haired old man looked out at them. He was dressed in a linen coat and black trousers and was obviously a manservant.

'I'm Mr Carpenter and this is Miss Morgan,' Alec said. The old man looked short-sightedly at them, then pulled the door wide open.

'Come in, sir! I didn't hear the engine of the taxi,' he said, peering past them into the snowy darkness.

'You didn't hear it because the taxi driver wouldn't bring us up to the house,' Alec said sharply. 'He said if he tried to get up the drive he might get stuck and be there for the night.'

The old man, tut-tutting and shaking his white head, led them into the big-oak-panelled hall. Sally gave a gasp of pleasure seeing the big log fire burning in the open grate and the gaily decorated and illuminated Christmas tree which stood at the bottom of the wide staircase. She heard Alec's exclamation and knew he was as taken aback as she was.

'I'm sure you'd like to go to your rooms,' the old servant said. 'I'll take you along, sir, and Mildred will take the young lady.'

As he spoke, a rosy-cheeked girl in cap and apron came smilingly forward. She took Sally's suitcase and started up the stairs.

'The other young lady and gentleman have already arrived,' Sally heard the old manservant say.

She caught Alec's eye, and he shrugged. Obviously he was as puzzled as she was as to whom the old man was referring to.

Soon Sally was being shown into a big bedroom full of well polished but very old-fashioned furniture. The heavy green curtains and the patterned carpet were rather dismal but these were offset by a cheerful fire burning in the grate, and two lamps with rose-coloured shades which filled the room with a warm soft light.

'Dinner's at eight o'clock, miss,' the maid said, after showing Sally where the bathroom was. 'Will you want me to help you to unpack?'

But Sally shook her head with a smile. 'No, thank you, Mildred, I'll manage. But you might run me a bath. I feel it would help me to thaw out.'

She slipped out of her clothes and into a dressing-gown, then went along to the bathroom where a steaming bath awaited her. For the next ten minutes she lay in the hot water wondering what lay ahead of her in the next few days. Already things had turned out very differently from what she had expected. First, she had not thought there would be anybody else spending Christmas at Monk's Hollow but herself. Apart from Alec Carpenter there were evidently at least two other people, judging from what the manservant had said.

And Monk's Hollow itself! It was very different from the house she had expected Aunt Agatha to live in. True, it was an old rather spooky place, but the log fire and the Christmas tree and the general air of comfort were all unexpected.

When she had dried herself on a big, fleecy bath-towel, Sally went back to her room. Suddenly she felt over-poweringly

25

sleepy. The bed looked very tempting and she lay on it, covering herself with the thick eiderdown. She felt wonderfully comfortable and drowsy. There was no hurry. If she lay here for half an hour or so she could dress in a leisurely fashion and go downstairs...

She wakened with a start. How long had she been asleep? She glanced at her wristwatch and saw with dismay that it was almost seven o'clock. She must have been asleep for well over an hour!

She jumped up and began to take her things out of her suitcase. She chose a simple blue dress with a pleated skirt which she had bought for an office party a few months before. It contrasted with her fair hair and exactly matched the blue of her eyes.

When she had done her hair and had fastened the string of pearls which had been her mother's round her slender neck she looked into the mirror. She wondered what Alec Carpenter would think of her when he saw her? So far he had only seen her huddled in a heavy coat with snow in her hair.

When she was ready she left the room and went down a passage along which

Mildred had brought her. They had seemed to come round several corners and when she came to two passages—one going to the left and one to the right—she hesitated, not quite sure which to take.

She decided to go to the right and walked along this corridor past a number of closed doors. Soon she began to doubt whether she was going in the right direction. Surely she should have reached the main staircase by this time.

She stopped and looked round. Had she better go back and start again? But before she could make up her mind she heard the sound of weeping just ahead of her. She frowned. Who could this be? Perhaps it was one of the servants. Ought she to go further along the passage and see if there was anything she could do to help?

As she stood there a thin figure in what appeared to be a grey cowl came round a corner, a few yards ahead of her, weeping and wringing its hands. This phantom-like form came a few yards towards her, then suddenly seemed to disappear into the wall.

Sally was almost overcome with a desire to turn on her heel and run for her life.

Then she told herself not to be a fool. There must be some explanation of where the woman had gone to.

She went forward again and saw, on her left, a narrow staircase which ran up into the darkness above. Could the woman have gone up here? If she had she had disappeared very quickly from sight.

Suddenly panic swept over Sally. Turning on her heel she ran back down the dimly lit passage the way she had come.

The other passage turned out to be the right one and soon she was standing at the top of the wide staircase looking down at the gaily lit Christmas tree and the blazing log fire below. She stood for a moment while her breathing quietened and she felt the warmth creeping back into her chilled limbs.

Then slowly she went down the stairs, hesitated in the hall for a moment or two, then turned towards a door behind which she heard the muted sound of laughter. Alec Carpenter, who was talking to a young man and woman sitting before a roaring fire, turned as she entered. His pleasant square-chinned face lit up, seeing her.

'Hello there, Sally!' he cried. 'Come and meet Mr Carley and Miss Renton.'

A good-looking young man who looked a year or two younger than Alec, rose from his chair with a smile and held out his hand. He was dressed in a well cut dark suit; he had smiling brown eyes and crisp well-brushed black hair.

The girl, who did not get up as Sally came forward to shake hands with Trevor Carley, had light green eyes and a pale beautiful face. Very red lips, curved into a smile as Sally came towards her, though the expression of her watching green eyes did not seem to change. Her very fair hair seemed almost white under the electric lights. It was piled bouffant style above her smooth forehead.

'How do you do,' she murmured, holding Sally's hand for a moment.

'Miss Renton's father was your Aunt Agatha's business partner,' Alec explained. 'She was asked to come here by your aunt for Christmas and bring her fiancé with her.'

'I was never more surprised in my life than when I received Mrs Pentland's letter,' Helen Renton said in a light, rather high-pitched voice. 'Actually, Trevor and

I had decided to go to the coast to an hotel for Christmas, but—well, I thought the old lady must be lonely or something if she wanted my company. Anyway, here we are.'

Sally, looking at the white shoulders rising from the sleeveless black dress, felt sure the thought of easing the loneliness of an old woman, had never entered this girl's head. However, she smiled politely, then looked round as the door opened and the manservant who had admitted her and Alec to the house some time before, entered the room. He was carrying a tray of drinks and he approached the little group by the fireplace.

'Sherry, or dry Martini, miss?' he asked, standing in front of Helen Renton.

She took a glass and he turned to Sally who asked for sherry. When the young men had helped themselves he made for the door again. Sally, suddenly remembering the woman whom she had met in such distress in the passage upstairs, called after him: 'Just a moment!' and when the old man turned towards her: 'When I was coming down a few minutes ago I took the wrong turning. I met a woman dressed in something that looked like a grey cowl. She was crying bitterly, though when she saw me she seemed to slip up some side stairs. I wonder if you know anything about her–'

The old man gave a little gasp as the colour faded from his cheeks. The heavy tray he carried fell to the carpet with a clatter. For a moment he stood there, his mouth working as if he was trying to say something, then turning away he hurried from the room, slamming the door behind him.

Sally looked at the others in astonishment.

'I seem to have upset him,' she said.

'He certainly looked as if he'd seen a ghost,' Trevor Carley cried.

But Helen Renton shook her head. With her pale green eyes fixed on Sally she said in a low voice:

'I should have said it looked more as if he thought Miss Morgan had seen one.'

3

Aunt Agatha

'But I don't believe in ghosts!' Sally looked round a little defiantly. 'The woman I saw could have been a servant who was upset about something and was going to her room. There was a little staircase leading out of the passage. She must have gone up it.'

Her voice trailed away, realising that the others were not listening to her.

Seeing that they were looking towards the door she turned her head in that direction.

The door was now standing open. Two people were looking into the room. One of them was an old woman seated in a wheel-chair. The other, a tall forbidding figure in black, stood behind the chair as if about to wheel it into the room.

The old woman, black eyes flashing, looked from one to the other of the little group about the fire. She had snow-white hair, beautifully dressed, above her thin, high cheek-boned face. She was dressed in grey silk. The voluminous skirt completely hid her legs and feet. In her right hand she carried a thin ebony cane, and as she looked at Sally she rapped sharply with it on one of the wheels of the chair.

'What nonsense is this you are talking!' she cried. 'Ghosts! Are you inferring that Monk's Hollow is haunted?'

Sally bit her lip. This must be her Aunt Agatha.

'You mustn't have heard what I was saying,' she said quietly. 'When I was coming down from my room earlier I saw what appeared to be a woman in distress. She seemed to disappear into the wall but when I looked I noticed a little staircase—'

'You must have a very vivid imagination, my child!' the old woman interrupted. 'Some of the passages in this old house are not very well lighted and what you saw must have been a shadow.'

Sally was about to burst out in her own defence but at that moment she felt a firm hand close over her elbow. She bit back the angry words that had come to her lips, glad that Alec Carpenter, by her side, had realised that nothing was to be gained by a senseless wrangle with the old woman.

'Mrs Pentland?' Alec asked, with a pleasant smile. 'I'm Alec Carpenter.'

The old woman nodded and glanced over her shoulder at the impassive figure behind.

'All right, Martin, wheel me into the room!' she snapped.

The middle-aged woman standing behind the chair, pushed it forward, then closed the door behind her. Agatha Pentland, resting her bony hands on the top of her cane—hands whose fingers were encrusted with diamond rings—looked up into Alec Carpenter's good-natured face.

'So you're my old friend's son, are you?' She nodded her head as if pleased with what she saw. 'Welcome to Monk's Hollow, Mr Carpenter. I hope you'll spend a very pleasant Christmas with me.'

'I'm sure I will, ma'am,' Alec said, then added: 'I hope you'll call me Alec. Mr Carpenter seems a very formal way of addressing your old friend's son.'

The old woman nodded with a smile then turned to Sally.

'You must be my niece!' For several seconds she looked Sally over, as if not sure that she liked what she saw or not. At last, as the colour began to burn into Sally's cheeks as her indignation grew, she said: 'Yes, you favour my side of the family, I'm glad to say. You've got your father's eyes and, judging by the expression on your face, some of his temper, too.'

Before Sally could say anything she turned abruptly to Helen Renton. 'I was glad when you said you could come to spend Christmas with me and bring your fiancé along as well,' she said with a little smile. 'My husband and your father were great friends as well as business partners. I was very sorry to hear the news that your father had died.'

Helen Renton produced a little handkerchief and dabbed at her eyes as if the old woman's words had affected her deeply.

'I know that Daddy was very fond of Mr Pentland,' she said, a trifle unsteadily. 'When he died Mr Pentland was very generous, even though at that time Daddy had ceased to be his partner. I was able to stay at school longer than would have been the case otherwise.'

The old woman fixed her eyes on Trevor Carley. She looked him over, her lips pursed, her eyes giving nothing away. At last she said:

'So you're going to marry this young woman, are you? How long have you been engaged?'

'Only a month, Mrs Pentland,' the young man replied. 'As Helen probably told you she came to work for me about three months ago. I'm employed by a small manufacturing business and Helen took the job as my secretary.'

'I thought you were on the stage,' Mrs Pentland exclaimed, looking back at Helen.

Helen gave a rather shrill little laugh.

'I was on the stage for a few months,' she admitted, 'but it's awfully hard getting work. When I'd been out of a job for several weeks I decided to benefit from the secretarial course I took soon after leaving school. You may remember, Mrs Pentland, your husband paid for it. It was just one of the kind things he did for me before he died.'

The old lady sat for several seconds staring straight before her. It was obvious that she was thinking of the man who seemed to have won so completely Helen Renton's gratitude. Suddenly, as if realising

36

that the four young people were watching her curiously, she smiled round at them, then glanced over her shoulder at the woman behind the chair.

'Martin, go and see where Briggs has got to!' she ordered. 'He knows I like a glass of sherry at this time.'

As the woman, still without uttering a word, turned away and left the room, Mrs Pentland looked back at her guests. 'You are all here save one,' she said. 'I imagine he must have been held up in the snow. However, no doubt he'll turn up in due course.'

Sally wondered who her aunt could be referring to. Obviously it was a man. But was he young or old? She smiled at herself. Why should she be so interested? In any case the man would be putting in an appearance very shortly and she would be able to see for herself.

The door opened and the old manservant came in with another tray of drinks. Mrs Pentland took a glass of sherry. Trevor Carley, who had finished his first drink, helped himself to another dry Martini.

The old lady raised her glass. 'I hope you have a very good Christmas,' she said. 'I think, as this seems an appropriate moment, I should explain to you why I have invited you here.'

She looked from one intent face to another, her dark eyes in her pale face tinged with something that might have been sadness. Sally's heart quickened. All along, ever since she had received Aunt Agatha's letter, she had wondered why she had been commanded—you could hardly call it invited—to Monk's Hollow for Christmas. Now the reason was going to come out at last.

'I am a fairly wealthy woman,' Agatha Pentland said in a low voice. 'I am also quite alone in the world. True, I have one relative—' for a moment her eyes rested on Sally, 'but she is a stranger to me. I met her for the first time, as you know, a few minutes ago. If I die without making a will my niece, as my next of kin, would automatically come in for a fortune. I don't intend that to happen!'

Sally felt the colour burn up into her cheeks again. What an awful old woman Aunt Agatha was! She made it sound very much as if she, her niece, had lived for years in expectation of coming into her money, when, in actual fact, she had never so far given it a thought.

For the second time that evening angry words came to her lips, and once more a firm kindly hand closed over her arm.

'Steady, Sally!' Alec Carpenter said in a low voice.

Sally flashed him a quick smile. He was quite right. There was nothing to be gained by losing her temper. She might as well listen to what the old woman had to say.

'I spoke to my solicitor the other day,' Mrs Pentland said, a note of weariness now creeping into her voice. 'I explained that I was inviting my niece, the son of my best friend, the daughter of my partner—and one other—to spend Christmas with me here at Monk's Hollow. I said that I wanted to get to know my guests and that, at the end of the holiday, I would make my will, either leaving the money to one of you or—if none of you impressed me—to some charity I shall ask my solicitor to choose for me.'

Alec, by Sally's side, drew a sharp breath.

'But, Mrs Pentland, I hardly feel that I am entitled to—' he began, but quickly she interrupted:

'And why not? Your mother, until she died, was my very dearest friend. I shall always be grateful to her for the love and kindness she gave me so unselfishly.'

She smiled at him. 'Whether I shall take to her son as much as I loved her—well, we shall have to wait and see.'

Sally caught sight of Trevor Carley's face. There was a worried frown on his forehead as he leaned towards Helen Renton and whispered something to her. She frowned as she listened and Sally decided that whatever it was her fiancé was saying it was not pleasing her too well.

Suddenly the young man said: 'I think my fiancée agrees with me, Mrs Pentland, that she has no right to any of your money. After all, though her father was in partnership with your late husband, he had left the firm some time before he died. Mr Pentland was kindness itself to Helen. I'm sure she agrees with me that it would be quite wrong for her to benefit any more in the circumstances.'

The old lady, her hands resting on the top of her cane, smiled at the young man and nodded approvingly.

'Your sentiments do you great credit, young man,' she said. 'But please allow me to know my own business best. Of course, it is possible that I may not leave a penny to your fiancée, in which case no one will be any the worse, but I would certainly like her to take her chance with the others. What do you say about that yourself, Helen?'

Helen bit her lip and cast an uncertain smile at the young man by her side.

'You're very kind, Mrs Pentland,' she murmured. 'But as Trevor says—'

Sally, watching her closely, wondered at her real feelings. The tightening of the other girl's lips, the unguarded look that had come into her eyes when her fiancé had spoken out, had, just for a moment, given away how furious she was that this man she was to marry had chosen to try to queer her pitch with this rich old woman.

A little impatiently Agatha Pentland drank the last of her sherry and handed her glass to her attendant.

'Thank you, my dear,' she said, glancing at Helen again. 'I would prefer you to leave things as they are. I take it that I can depend on you?'

With a little sigh which could have been one of relief, Helen nodded.

'You're very kind,' she murmured and, for a moment, her eyes left the old lady's face and fell on the frail hands resting on the ebony stick.

Just for a moment Sally, watching her, wondered if this other girl was assessing the value of the rings on the old lady's hands, wondering how they would look on her own slender fingers, calculating what they would fetch if she sold them.

Then she told herself not to be so unfair. What did she really know about this other girl, Helen Renton? For all she knew she might be a kind and generous girl who really did feel that she should not be included in Aunt Agatha's plans for making a will.

Before she could think any more on these lines there was a knock on the door and the old manservant looked in.

'Yes, Briggs, what is it?' Mrs Pentland asked sharply.

But before the old man could speak he was pushed firmly to one side and a tall broad-shouldered young man came into the room and smiled round at those present.

4

The Newcomer

'I'm Colin Brent!' the newcomer said.

'So there you are at last!' The old lady's face lit up as she turned. She held out her hand and the young man went quickly forward to take it. 'I suppose the storm is worse than ever?'

'It certainly is!' The young man lifted the beringed hand to his lips. 'You must be Mrs Pentland who sent me that kind letter. It was good of you to invite me here for Christmas. I fully appreciate your courtesy, Madam.'

Sally, watching this little scene, wondered where she had seen this young man before. He was very good-looking with his regular features, his square chin, his crisp fair hair and his well-proportioned body. He was dressed in well-cut tweeds which, on another man, would have been considered loud but which, on his athletic frame, were just right. He had very blue eyes and he turned these on Agatha Pentland as if she was the only person in the whole world that he had any interest in.

He's a professional charmer, all right, Sally thought, then, quite by chance, caught sight of Helen Renton's face as she too looked at the newcomer. She was looking at Colin Brent as if she had seen a ghost; her hands were tightly clenched at her side and she was biting on her soft red underlip as if to steady its trembling. Her eyes had a stunned disbelieving look, as if she could not quite credit what they saw.

'And now I must introduce you to my other guests,' Aunt Agatha said. 'This is my niece, Sally Morgan.'

Sally felt her hand taken in a big warm grasp as the blue eyes turned on her and even white teeth flashed in a friendly smile.

'How do you do, Miss Morgan?' Colin Brent asked, and suddenly Sally knew where she had seen him before.

Her landlady, Mrs Best, had a television set, and sometimes she asked Sally down in the evening if there was a good play on. About four weeks ago she had seen this man take a part in a thriller which she had enjoyed. He had been a man about town who was also a jewel thief.

'I've seen you on television,' she said impulsively.

He grinned at her. 'How nice it is to be famous! It saves so much explanation.'

'Colin's father was well known on the stage though he's been dead some years,' Aunt Agatha announced to the room at large.

'Was he Laurence Brent?' Trevor Carley asked.

The actor nodded. 'Yes, he died five years ago. I'm so glad he's still remembered.'

'And why shouldn't he be remembered?' the old lady demanded sharply. 'He was quite famous. I followed his career for—many years.'

Sally watched curiously as Colin approached Helen Renton. But the other girl had regained her composure by this time. She held out her hand and he took it with a little smile.

'Good evening, Miss Renton,' he said, almost in an off-hand manner, then turned to Alec Carpenter as the old lady said the New Zealander's name.

Briggs, the manservant, now appeared

with a drink for the newcomer. Colin Brent held up his glass and smiled at the old lady.

'Here's wishing you the very best of health, Madam' he said. 'It was nice of you to invite me to spend Christmas with you. I would have had a very lonely time otherwise.'

'I think I'd better tell you that I had an ulterior motive in asking you and these other young people here,' Agatha Pentland said.

Briefly she told him about the will she was about to make and how she would choose her heir from Sally, Helen, Alec or himself.

'I'm deeply grateful to you, dear lady, for your consideration for me,' Colin Brent declared in his rather old fashioned way, 'but I don't quite see—'

'There's a very good reason for my including you in this little house-party,' Mrs Pentland said with a smile. Then, looking over her shoulder she said sharply: 'I'm tired, Martin. I must go up to my room now. I'll have some dinner sent up.'

As the attendant opened the door preparatory to wheeling the chair out into the hall, the old lady looked round once more.

'I hope you have a very happy first dinner together in my house,' she said. 'I'm only sorry that I'm too tired to preside. I will see you all tomorrow morning.'

With a curt nod she was wheeled away. As the door closed behind her Colin Brent gave a long whistle of relief and sank into a chair.

'My, but I'm glad to sit down!' he declared. 'My car packed it in about a mile from Monk's Hollow and I had to finish the journey on foot. Lugging a ruddy great suitcase as well, I might add.'

Trevor Carley laughed. 'It's good to hear you speaking the King's English! I thought when I heard you talking to Mrs Pentland that you'd stepped straight out of a Victorian novel.'

The other winked solemnly. 'Oh, that's the line I take with all the old ladies! They love it, you know.'

Sally couldn't help but smile at this. There was no doubt in her mind that this Colin Brent was an adventurer but he was a likeable scamp for all that. Undoubtedly the party at Monk's Hollow this Christmas would be a good deal brighter with him as part of it than if he had not come at all.

Presently Briggs appeared to announce dinner. Sally and Helen led the way across the hall to the big, rather gloomy dining-room. One end of the long table had been laid with five places. As odd man out Colin Brent took the head of the table with Sally and Alec on his left and Helen and Trevor on his right. He looked round at them with an amused smile.

'I take it that your invitations to come to Monk's Hollow for Christmas were as much a bolt out of the blue as mine was?' he asked.

No one spoke for several seconds, then Sally nodded.

'I'd never heard from my aunt before,' she said. 'She quarrelled with my father many years ago. The first time I ever heard from her was a few days ago when she told me to come down here for Christmas.'

Trevor Carley looked at her in astonishment.

'Do you mean to say that she never once got in touch with her only relative?'

Sally shook her head. 'She made no attempt to get in touch with either my father or me when my father was alive. When he died I disappeared. I wanted to make a new start and I went into digs. If she tried to get in touch with me then I never heard about it.'

'But how did she find you when she wrote to you?' Helen asked curiously.

'She must have had someone looking for me, spying on me, if you like,' Sally said a little bitterly. 'They probably found me a long time ago but she didn't get in touch with me until earlier this week.'

'She's certainly a strange woman in many ways,' Alec said slowly. 'But I have an advantage over you other folk. You see, I've been through all the letters Mrs Pentland wrote to my mother, who was her best friend. She's not the callous hard-hearted creature her treatment of Sally would lead you to believe. In fact, in some of her letters she expresses regret that the quarrel with her nephew was never made up.'

Colin Brent looked at Helen by his side. There was a little smile on his lips when he spoke.

'And what connection have you with Mrs Pentland, Miss—er—Renton?' he asked.

Helen, flushing, avoided his eyes. Slowly she said:

'At one time my father was in partnership

with Mrs Pentland's husband. But Daddy left the firm and went into business on his own. Then he fell ill and died. I was surprised to be invited here by the old lady. After all, she has no responsibility towards me now.'

The meal was beautifully cooked and skilfully served by Briggs and the maid who had shown Sally up to her room earlier. There was champagne and though Sally only sipped at the golden wine in her glass the others, especially Colin, drank it with pleasure. The young actor, indeed, made no effort to stop Briggs refilling his glass from time to time as the well-cooked meal proceeded through its various courses.

'Goose, eh!' Colin declared as a well-filled plate was put in front of him. 'I suppose we'll get the turkey tomorrow!'

He laughed, but the others did not join in. Sally, glancing sideways at Alec, saw that he was frowning. Undoubtedly he thought that the other young man's remark had been in poor taste.

'You know, I can't help wondering why the old lady invited me here,' Colin said, sipping at his newly-filled glass. 'I don't mind telling you I'm very glad to be here, as a matter of fact. TV's an excellent thing—I prefer it to the stage—but engagements are few and far between. If the old girl hadn't sent her invitation I'd have had a pretty thin time this Christmas. Certainly I shouldn't have been drinking champagne as excellent as this!'

The others looked uncomfortably at each other. It was obvious that the actor had had more champagne than was wise.

Trevor Carley looked across the table at Alec and tried to change the subject by asking him when he had arrived in England. Alec told him and answered some general questions about life in New Zealand. Sally stole a glance at the figure at the head of the table. Colin Brent seemed to be deep in thought but, suddenly catching her eye, he slapped his hand hard down on the polished surface, startling everybody.

'I've got it!' he cried. 'I've just remembered something my mother told me when I was only a small boy. Apparently when my father was something of a matinée idol, all the girls used to fall in love with him. He was a bachelor at that time and I suppose he made hay while the sun shone. Anyhow, one girl must have been a bit brighter than the rest for, according to my mother, the old man got engaged. But it mustn't have worked out for, shortly afterwards, the engagement was broken off. Years passed, then when my father found himself in a play with my mother, they fell in love and were married shortly afterwards. I was born when my father was in his late forties—he was middle-aged when he married my mother—and I wonder, bearing in mind that my father would have been in his seventies if he'd been alive today, if that first girl he was engaged to might not have been—Agatha Pentland!'

'Why don't you ask her?' Helen asked him a little sharply, turning her green eyes on him.

He nodded solemnly. 'I think I will. It certainly seems a likely explanation as to why I was invited here.'

'But I can't see, if your father jilted Mrs Pentland, as seems likely, why she should be interested in his son,' Trevor said in a puzzled voice.

Colin Brent fixed him with a rather glassy eye. Taking a cigarette from the box old Briggs held out to him he flicked his lighter and blew smoke towards the ceiling.

'You have no imagination, my boy,' he declared. 'Suppose my father had married Agatha Pentland, the odds are that I would have come along just the same. In fact, I suppose the romantic old girl had got it into her head that if things had been different I would have been her son. It seems a feasible explanation to me. What do you others think?'

He looked round at their startled faces, then, when none of them spoke, he got unsteadily to his feet, swaying slightly, glass raised.

'I give you a toast,' he said, clutching at the end of the table to steady himself. 'To Agatha Pentland's heir—whoever he or she might be!'

5

A Confidential Talk

When dinner was over the five young people returned to the comfortable drawing-room for coffee. There was a big fire and sitting before it Sally soon began to feel overpoweringly sleepy.

Checking a yawn she caught Alec's eye. He grinned at her. 'Tired?'

She nodded. 'I was up very early this morning. It seems to have been a pretty full day.'

'I think we'd all benefit by an early night,' Trevor put in. 'What do you say, dear?'

Helen, who had seemed deep in thought, started at her fiancé's question. She forced a smile.

'I'm ready for bed if everyone else is,' she replied.

'How about you, Brent?' Alec asked, looking across at the actor who was sunk into one of the big armchairs. He gave a little laugh. 'He looks as if he'd gone to bed already! He's fast asleep.'

Colin Brent, as if conscious that they were looking at him, opened his eyes and looked round at them in a bemused way.

'I must have dropped off for a moment,' he muttered. 'I—I hope the ladies will forgive me.'

Sally got to her feet. 'I think I'll go up now,' she said. 'Good night all.'

But the others said they would go with her and followed her out into the hall. As she reached the top of the wide staircase Sally saw the middle-aged woman who seemed to be her aunt's personal servant standing there. Sally smiled.

'Good night,' she said, but the woman shook her head.

'Mrs Pentland would like to see you before you retire, Miss Morgan,' she said in a surprisingly soft voice for such a forbidding-looking woman. 'Will you come with me, please?'

The others, who had followed Sally upstairs, heard the words and exchanged glances. But Sally ignored them.

'Perhaps you'll lead the way,' she said to the woman who, without more ado, started off along the corridor leading in the opposite direction from Sally's room.

Sally looked at the broad back and erect head of the woman walking a few feet ahead of her. Was Martin a nurse, a companion, or simply her aunt's personal maid? Whatever she was she was obviously unfriendly and uncommunicative. Perhaps Aunt Agatha had chosen her for these very qualities.

She's certainly not the kind of person I'd want around all the time if I lived in a lonely house deep in the country, Sally thought, then slowed up as the woman came to a halt outside a door. Raising her hand she knocked gently.

'Come in!'

Sally heard the faint voice behind the thick panels. The woman opened the door and ushered her into the room.

'Here's Miss Morgan, Madam,' she said to the white-haired figure sitting propped against pillows in the big four-poster against the wall at the far end of the big bedroom.

'Thank you, Martin.' Mrs Pentland said. 'You can go to bed now. I'd like to talk to my niece alone.'

Just for a moment Sally met the cold grey eyes in the square unattractive face, then the woman turned on her heel and went from the room, pulling the door to behind her.

'Come over here, niece!' the old lady said imperiously, indicating a chair at the side of the bed.

Sally went forward. Her feet sank into the thick pile of the richly patterned carpet. The heavy wine-red velvet curtains and the massive mahogany furniture spoke of a period long before Sally was born. A fire was burning in the old-fashioned grate; the

56

air was warm and stuffy, and smelt faintly of cigarette smoke. Sally found herself wondering who smoked—the grim-faced attendant or her mistress.

As if in answer to her unspoken question the old lady groped for something on an occasional table by her side. A moment later she was lighting a cigarette and leaning back against her pillows to regard Sally through eyes half-closed against the smoke.

'I suppose you'd rather be going to bed than sitting here talking to me, eh?' she said after a little silence.

Sally forced a smile. 'Not at all,' she said politely. 'I'm glad to have an opportunity of getting to know you better.'

The old lady digested this for some time in silence, puffing at her cigarette until the end glowed red. At last she said:

'I was sorry when I heard that your father had died. I was very fond of him, very fond indeed.'

Sally bit back the angry words that came to her lips. There was no sense in losing her temper right away. Best to hear what the old lady had to say first.

'I was certainly surprised that I didn't hear from you after the solicitor told you about my father dying,' she said quietly.

The old lady nodded. 'It may surprise you to hear that I didn't learn of your father's death until some time after his funeral. I was out of the country at the time. I had been ill and my doctor had persuaded me to go to a warmer climate for the winter. When I returned to this country and tried to get in touch with you, you had apparently disappeared, and no one knew where you were.'

Sally had to admit to herself that this explanation was quite reasonable. It certainly explained why her aunt had not got in touch with her after her father's death.

'I suppose you're wondering how I finally got in touch with you?' Mrs Pentland asked. 'When I found you had disappeared I put enquiry agents on your trail but it was a full six months before they caught up with you. By that time I was again wintering abroad and it was not until this Christmas, which my doctor allowed me to spend at Monk's Hollow, that I was able to issue an invitation for you to come here.'

Sally, looking into the tired old face, felt a sudden stab of pity. Whatever Aunt Agatha had done in the past was over now.

It seemed a pity to keep an ancient feud alive, especially at Christmas time.

There was more curiosity than bitterness in her voice when she asked:

'Why did you dislike my mother so much, Aunt Agatha? She was a very sweet person and she made my father very, very happy.'

For some time the old lady did not reply. Her eyes were fixed on the flickering flames in the grate as if she expected them to provide an answer to the question she had been asked.

'I had such wonderful plans for your father,' she said at last in a voice that was little more than a whisper. 'I brought him up, as you know, after his mother and father were killed in that accident soon after they were married. I never had any children of my own'—the old voice faltered for a moment, then went on, slower than before—'I had only been married a short time to Mr Pentland. Your father was a dear little boy and when no children of my own came along I gave him all my love. Mr Pentland was a kind man but he was also a very busy one and I saw little of him. Your father grew up and I had great plans for him. He could have

59

made an excellent marriage with any of the daughters of well-to-do business men Mr Pentland used to bring home. But he chose to go his own way. He wouldn't follow Mr Pentland in the business but preferred to take an ill-paid job somewhere else. Then—then he married your mother and—well, I was bitterly disappointed by this time and washed my hands of him.'

'I can understand you being disappointed after all your hopes,' Sally said, 'but need you have kept it up over the years?'

The old lady allowed herself a rather bitter little smile.

'You don't know everything, child,' she said wearily. 'You see, your father and I were very similar in character. I was angry with him for marrying your mother, he was angry with me for being angry. Neither of us would budge an inch. When your mother died I wrote to him and hoped that the breach might be healed. But he would have none of it! He wrote me a letter that left me in no doubt that he never wanted either to see or hear from me again. It was the letter of a despairing grief-stricken man who had lost the thing he treasured most in all the world.'

The feeble old voice died away and the

only sound in the room was the faint crackle of the fire in the grate. Sally, seeing that Aunt Agatha's eyes had closed, got quietly to her feet. It would perhaps be best if she slipped away, leaving the old lady to rest. She had a great deal to think over and the sooner she got back to her own room the better.

But as she tiptoed across the carpet towards the door, Aunt Agatha's voice called faintly after her:

'Perhaps you see now, Sally, that all the fault wasn't on my side. I did want you to understand that. I know you must have hated me all these years but—well, the older I get the more I realise that hate is an emotion one can't afford to indulge in.'

Sally looked round with a smile. 'Go to sleep, now, Aunt Agatha. Perhaps we can have another talk tomorrow.'

The old lady closed her eyes with a sigh and said something that might have been 'Good night'. Sally, opening the door of the room, stepped out into the corridor and turned towards her own room. As she passed the top of the stairs she looked down and saw that the Christmas tree below had been switched off and that only a small lamp, which cast a pool of shadow, was burning in the hall.

She supposed that everybody was in bed and she hurried along the dimly-lit corridor towards her own room, her feet making no sound on the thick carpet.

Then suddenly, as she was about to turn the corner, she heard the whisper of voices just ahead of her. She wondered who it could be. Perhaps it was a couple of servants who had met in the corridor on their way to bed.

Then she distinctly heard a man's voice say: 'Oh, come off it, Helen! You can't expect me to swallow that!'

Sally drew a sharp breath. So Colin Brent, as soon as Trevor Carley was safely in his room, had sought out his fiancée and was now evidently renewing a friendship which both he and Helen had chosen to keep secret earlier that evening.

Standing there Sally heard Helen's agitated whisper: 'The last time I saw you I let you see pretty plainly that I never wanted to set eyes on you again.'

With an amused chuckle the man said: 'You can hardly blame me for being here for Christmas, my dear. I'd no idea you'd be one of the party.'

'Even if you had known you'd still have come!' Helen said angrily. 'It would take a pack of wild wolves to keep you away from the possibility of inheriting any money. I wasn't engaged to you for three months not to have found that out.'

So that explained Helen's dismay when Colin Brent had arrived tonight, Sally thought. Perhaps she had told her new fiancé that she had never been in love with anybody else until he came along. Colin Brent would take some explaining away!

Lowering his voice Colin Brent said in a whisper Sally could hardly catch: 'We must be sensible about the old girl's money, Helen. You inferred that I'm always looking after Number One. Well, I can return the compliment with interest, knowing you a hundred times better than that dreary fellow you've got yourself engaged to. Why don't we talk things over sensibly? I think it would be better to work together than against each other.'

'You must go now, Colin,' Helen said agitatedly. 'I think I hear someone coming. Good night.'

It was an obvious excuse to get rid of him. Sally heard the click of the closing door, then, to her relief Colin Brent, after a moment's hesitation, walked down the corridor away from her. After standing there for a few more seconds she went cautiously on her way, reaching her room without further incident.

6

An Alarming Experience

It was some time before Sally fell asleep. So much had happened that day that her mind whirled round and round with all she had heard and experienced.

But at last she fell asleep, only to jerk awake with the heavy darkness pressing in on her and an utter conviction that she was not alone in the room.

She lay there, paralysed with fear. Cold air seemed to be blowing on her face as if the window was open. She strained to see through the darkness, but not a glimmer of light came through the thick curtains. The door, she knew, had been fast shut when she went to sleep.

She lay listening. If there was anyone in the room they would surely make a move and she would hear them.

But not a sound came to her straining ears. She thought of the bedside lamp and very slowly, hardly daring to breathe, she slipped her arm from under the covers and stretched out to put the light on.

Then suddenly, without warning, a cold hand passed lightly over her face. She sank back against the pillows petrified with fear. Once again the ice-cold fingers touched her brow, her cheeks, her chin.

She tried to scream but no sound passed her lips. The black darkness pressed in on her like a living thing, threatening to suffocate her.

Gasping, sobbing for breath, she turned on her side and groped wildly for the light. She thought she heard a sudden movement near the bed, then a click as if a door had closed.

At last her trembling hand found the light switch. A moment later the lamp was lit and she lay looking round with frightened eyes at the familiar sight of her room. There was nothing to be seen except the furniture and her clothes which she had folded on a chair before getting into bed. Whoever had been in the room a few seconds before had slipped away.

She supposed there was no lamp burning in the corridor outside which accounted for no light shining into the room when the door was opened. Getting out of bed she was surprised to find that her legs were trembling so violently that they would hardly support her. Somehow she reached the door and pulled it open.

A light almost outside the door shone in at her! Suddenly horror swept over her. Whoever had been in the room with her had not left by either the window or the door. Where had they gone then? Had they disappeared into thin air?

She looked over her shoulder into her room where the little lamp was burning by the side of the bed. She felt she could not go back in there and lie there waiting for the morning to come.

She took a couple of uncertain steps along the corridor, only knowing that she wanted to get away from the room and the terror she had known there, but as she moved forward the walls on either side of her seemed to tilt as the floor came up to meet her.

With a pitiful little cry she pitched

forward on to her face and lay still.

When she came to her head was resting against something solid and a pair of strong arms was supporting her.

'What is it? I heard you cry out and came to see what had happened!'

To her relief it was Alec Carpenter's voice. She found herself looking up into his kindly concerned eyes. She tried to struggle up but he held her so that she could not move.

'Take it easy!' he said. 'You must have fainted. In a moment or two I'll carry you back to your room. You should be in bed.'

'But—but I don't want to stay in my room,' she said a little wildly. 'It—it was because of what happened there that I ran out into the corridor.'

He frowned. 'I don't think I understand. What could have happened there? Did you have a nightmare?'

Suddenly she realised that the story she had to tell was a wildly improbable one. Though Alec Carpenter was kind and would undoubtedly listen to her he would certainly believe that she had imagined it all. Once again she struggled to get up. This time he helped her to her feet.

'Would you like me to get one of the servants up?' he asked. 'You look very white, as if you've had a nasty shock.'

But she shook her head. Just as, a few moments before, she had been so eager to get out of her room, she was now just as keen to return to it. She was even beginning to entertain doubts that the frightening experience she had gone through mightn't after all be imagination brought on by a bad dream.

'I'll be all right now,' she said, forcing a smile. But he insisted on accompanying her back to her room and seeing her tucked safely into bed again.

'What time is it?' she asked and he glanced at the watch on his wrist.

'Just after four o'clock.' He hesitated. 'Would you like me to sit with you until morning? I know what it's like to have nightmares. I used to suffer from them a lot as a boy.'

But she shook her head once again.

'No, I'd rather be by myself, if you don't mind. You're awfully kind but there's no reason why you should lose any more sleep. I'll be all right now.'

He looked at her uncertainly. Before he turned away at the door he looked back. 'I

68

think I'd leave that lamp burning for the rest of the night if I were you,' he said, and she nodded.

'I will! Good night, and thank you once again.' Then he was gone and she was lying back, staring up at the ceiling and wondering if she really had been a victim of an hallucination—or if someone had come into the room by some secret means to pass cold hands over her face, as a blind man might do, to discover what she looked like.

Sally shivered. However she tried to convince herself she was quite sure that she had neither imagined what had taken place nor had dreamed it. Someone really had got into this room and had left it as mysteriously as they had entered it.

She got out of bed and, crossing to the door, turned on the overhead light. Pulling on her dressing-gown she stood in the centre of the room and looked round. When she had first come into this room some hours before she had noticed the rather dismal green curtains and patterned carpet, and the massive old-fashioned furniture. The wardrobe alone was big enough to conceal two men.

The thought was a terrifying one and she

stood in front of the wardrobe wondering if she dare open its door. She saw herself reflected in the long mirror on the wall, a slim frightened figure with an apprehensive face, and suddenly she smiled. What a fool she was! Only earlier that evening she had put her dresses inside the wardrobe. She hadn't been frightened then; why should she be frightened now?

Seizing the handle she opened the door and looked into the deep interior. The light shone in on her few clothes hanging there. There was nothing else.

She examined the back of the huge piece of furniture but the craftsmen who had made it had intended it to last many, many years. The back of the wardrobe was a solid sheet of mahogany. There were no secret doors there!

Sally toured the room. For the first time she noticed that the walls were covered with a thick wine-coloured paper. She examined it carefully to see if the paper concealed any panelling, but nothing was visible.

Between the big dressing table and the window a long mirror had been let into the wall. Before dinner, when Sally had finished dressing, she had stood in front of this mirror and had examined herself critically. One of the few things she found unsatisfactory about her digs in London was that there was no long mirror she could use to see if the seams of her stockings were crooked or her slip was showing.

She wondered how long this mirror had been fixed to the wall. She examined it and saw that the screws were rusted into their sockets. That looked as if it had been there a good number of years.

She turned away, deciding to go back to bed. She was beginning to feel overpoweringly sleepy again. Obviously there was nothing to be gained by prowling round the room like this in the middle of the night. Then as a thought struck her, she turned back to the mirror. The frame stood away from the wall, perhaps half an inch, and she ran an exploratory finger over the smooth surface, first up the right hand side, then the left. But nothing happened.

As if I really expected anything would! she thought, then, because she knew she would not sleep until she had satisfied herself entirely, she reached on tiptoe and felt along the dusty ledge at the top of the mirror.

71

Her heart quickened. For her questing fingers had encountered a slight bulge which could have been a paint blister or—a button!

Holding her breath she pressed, then fell back in alarm as the long mirror opened outwards from the wall like a door. Sally, her limbs trembling uncontrollably, found herself looking with startled eyes into a narrow passage which disappeared into total darkness.

She felt a breath of cold dank air on her cheek and shivered. Now she knew where her visitor had come from.

On a sudden impulse she pushed the mirror back against the wall and heard the click as it closed. She looked round for something heavy she could put in front of the mirror so that it would not open again from the other side. But there was nothing suitable except for the wardrobe and dressing-table, and obviously she wasn't strong enough to move them.

Then her eye fell on the fire-irons, standing on the hearth. Picking these up she placed them in front of the mirror.

A few moments later she was lying in bed. If anyone opened the mirror now they would knock the fire-irons over with a clatter and she would wake. It was the best she could do until morning.

Though she was shivering from cold she soon grew warmer under the thick blankets. Her last thought before she fell asleep was: Shall I tell my aunt what has happened tonight, or shall I try to find out what is going on by myself?

7

Christmas Morning

The strains of 'Christians Awake' roused Sally in the morning.

For some time she lay trying to sort out the many confused thoughts that filled her mind. Suddenly she raised herself on her elbow and looked towards the long mirror on the wall. Seeing the fire-irons standing where she had put them in the night, everything flooded back.

She jumped out of bed and went to the window. Pulling the heavy curtains aside she found herself looking out on a white world. The sun was shining from a blue sky on to the snow thick on the trees, walls, and the lawns which ran away from the house.

Looking up at her window was a circle of expectant little faces, rosy in the morning light, their eyes alight with anticipation. The sound of the curtain being swished back had caught the children's attention. Seeing Sally looking out at them they turned rather self-consciously to the young woman, clad warmly in thick coat and head-scarf, who was obviously in charge of them, and burst into 'Good King Wenceslas'.

Sally pulled her dressing-gown on. As she listened to the sweet voices singing the old carol she found it hard to believe that last night's events had taken place.

The stifling darkness, the cold air on her face as she lay, paralysed with fear, in bed, the hand which had traced her features with chill fingers—all these were surely figments of her imagination.

She put the fire-irons back in the hearth and looked at the long mirror again. Beyond was a passageway down which her unknown visitor had come in the dead of night. Should she tell her aunt of the scare she had had? Or should she keep the story to herself for the time being?

As she dressed another thought struck her. Perhaps her aunt already knew about the secret passage. Perhaps—perhaps this was part of the old woman's plan to select her heir. Maybe the others—Alec, Helen, Colin Brent—had also been tested in some way. Perhaps the old lady would leave her money to the one who refused to panic, who refused to run away.

She compromised by deciding to say nothing to anybody for the time being. When she was dressed and had done her hair she looked out of the window again. She was just in time to see old Briggs, with a woollen comforter knotted about his thin throat, distributing Christmas cake to the group on the lawn below. As she watched Sally saw him give the young woman in charge of the children what appeared to be a pound note. A delighted smile came to her face, and, thanking the old man warmly, she said something to the children who, obediently, turned and followed her towards the corner of the house. Before they passed out of sight a little girl looked up at Sally's window and waved shyly.

Sally waved back, then glancing at her

watch and seeing that it was nearly half-past nine made for the door.

She found Alec and Trevor having breakfast. There was no sign of Helen and Colin. Alec jumped up, wished her a happy Christmas, and asked what he could get her from the massive carved sideboard where a number of dishes were keeping warm on a hot plate.

'Goodness, I'll never eat all this!' Sally gasped as presently he returned with a plateful of bacon and eggs.

'Of course you will!' As he put the plate before her he asked quietly, so that Trevor could not hear: 'Feeling OK?'

She nodded. 'Yes, thanks,' she said in a low voice, then a little louder: 'Did you hear the children singing?'

'Yes, it was wonderful! Apparently they go round the district every Christmas singing carols. They're the local school kids.'

'And what's the programme for today?' Trevor asked, buttering a piece of toast.

No one answered for at that moment Helen and Colin came into the room.

'Happy Christmas all!' Colin cried and beamed round as if filled with the spirit of goodwill.

Helen murmured something, refused anything but a slice of toast when Trevor suggested a kipper or bacon and eggs, and rather snappily pointed out to him that she drank coffee at breakfast time after he had poured and carried to her a cup of tea.

Sally noticed that Trevor did not say anything but that his lips tightened slightly. She also noticed that there was a little smile on Colin Brent's face as he helped himself at the sideboard as if the little scene had amused him.

Sally, as Alec, Colin and Trevor talked about other Christmases they had known, found herself wondering if it mightn't have been one of her companions who had visited her room during the night. After all, it would be to the advantage of all of them if she packed up and left Monk's Hollow. Even Trevor would benefit from Aunt Agatha's money—though she had not named him as a possible heir—for wasn't he to marry Helen?'

Then she remembered how she had overheard Helen and Colin talking together last night. Colin had suggested that their interests were the same and that they should act together. Suppose—suppose he or Helen had earlier found the entrance to the secret passage and had come along it to try, as the first phase in their campaign, to scare her so badly that she would go away.

That would only leave Alec, for Trevor could be ignored. He was not an heir and Helen, if she was working with Colin and still in love with him, would probably throw Trevor over without a qualm if she could only have Aunt Agatha's money by making a pact with Colin to share and share alike, whichever of them was the lucky one.

Yet—yet—looking from Helen's sulky face to Colin's cheerful one she couldn't really feel that she was on the right track. After all, Colin hadn't reached Monk's Hollow until late in the evening. He had certainly had little time to search for and find a secret passage, though Helen could have done so earlier and told him about it. But even that seemed doubtful.

The door opened and Martin, Aunt Agatha's servant, came into the room. She was dressed in black and her dark eyes glittered as, hands folded before her, she looked round at the young people sitting at the long table.

'I have a message from my mistress,' she

said, looking round. 'She intends to attend Morning Service at Darkling Church at eleven o'clock. She hopes her guests will accompany her.'

Then without another word she turned and left the room.

'Church!'

The word came as a gasp from Helen's lips. She looked round with such a look of consternation on her face that everybody burst out laughing.

'You make it sound as if we're being asked to go to prison,' Alec grinned, pouring himself more coffee. 'As a matter of fact, I'm rather glad. I hoped I'd be able to attend church at Christmas in England. It will be quite an experience for me.'

'Don't you have churches in New Zealand, then?' Colin Brent asked, a mischievous twinkle in his eyes.

'Yes, but not covered with snow and decorated with holly and mistletoe!'

'I suppose it will be something to do,' Trevor declared. 'I was wondering what sort of entertainment the old lady had in store for us on Christmas Day.'

'I hardly call it entertainment,' Helen grumbled. 'Besides, how are we to get there? The old lady hasn't mentioned

79

anything about a car, and Trevor's won't carry everybody. Yours is abandoned, isn't it?' she asked, glancing at Colin.

'Yes, as I told you last night I had to leave it in the snow. But what's wrong with us three'—he looked at Alec and Sally—'walking? It's a beautiful day. You two can take the old girl in Trevor's car.'

'I'd like that,' Sally said and Alec nodded enthusiastically.

'We'd better start getting ready,' he said. 'It's after ten now. Darkling is probably quite a distance away and the service starts at eleven.'

They made to leave the room but just then Briggs entered. He was dressed in a rusty old black coat and striped trousers. He cleared his throat before addressing the young men and the two girls.

'Madam asks me to say,' he began, 'that she will be driving to church in her car. There will be room for all.'

'But I have a car!' Trevor exclaimed after they had all exchanged surprised glances.

'She thinks it would perhaps be better if you went with her, sir,' Briggs said. 'She will meet you in the hall shortly after half-past ten.'

When the old man had gone Colin whistled.

'There are five of us and presumably she has a chauffeur!' he said. 'What sort of a contraption does she run: a charabanc?'

'It's time we went to get ready,' Sally said. 'See you in the hall!'

As she went upstairs Alec caught her up. His lean kindly face was concerned.

'Are you really all right, Sally?' he asked. 'You look a bit pale to me as if you didn't sleep much last night. You certainly seemed to have had a fright when I found you out in the corridor.'

'Alec!' She turned to look at him. They were in the quiet corridor which led to their rooms. 'Didn't you hear anything during the night?'

He frowned. 'Only you calling out. Should I have done?'

She shook her head. 'No, it was just that—'

'Just—what, Sally?' he demanded, putting out strong hands and gripping her arms. He looked down into her face. 'If anything's troubling you why don't you tell me about it?'

She bit her lip. She felt she could trust him fully, yet—yet perhaps it would be better if she made some more enquiries on her own before she confided in anyone.

'Everything's fine,' she said abruptly, and pulling away from him, ran into her room and closed the door behind her.

She stood back against the door, eyes closed, breathing quickly. Had she been a fool to rouse Alec's suspicions like that? Why had she inferred that something very mysterious had happened to her in the night? It would have been better, for the time being, to let him go on thinking she had just had a nightmare.

She dressed in her thick coat and a pair of stout shoes. She pulled a little fur cap she had made some weeks before over her fair hair and examined the result in the long wall mirror.

I look as if I'm going to the North Pole, she thought, then left the room and went downstairs to the hall.

A few minutes after half-past ten Aunt Agatha, helped by Mildred, the young maid, came downstairs. She walked with difficulty and supported herself heavily on her ebony stick. She was dressed in a sable coat of old fashioned cut with a plain black hat on her white hair.

There was a chorus of 'Happy Christmas!' as the old lady reached the hall and looked round.

'Thank you! I hope you all have one, too,' she replied. Then she glanced impatiently at the front door. 'Isn't the car here yet? Where can that woman have got to?'

Sally, who had been wondering why Mildred was deputising for Martin, turned as the door opened and the attendant came in from the driveway outside.

'I've brought the car round, Madam,' she said, crossing to Mrs Pentland's side. 'Shall I help you in?'

'Yes, we'll be late for service if we play about much longer,' the old lady said in a crotchety voice.

The young people held back until Mrs Pentland had been helped from the hall out into the snowy driveway. Here Sally, moving forward with the others, saw an ancient limousine standing before the front door. It was the biggest car she had ever seen.

'Gosh, what a hearse!' she heard Colin mutter at her side and she had to suppress a smile.

In a few moments Mrs Pentland had

been helped into the back of the old car. Martin glanced at the group by the door.

'Now, ladies and gentlemen,' she said. 'I think Mr Brent had better come in front with me and the young ladies and the other young gentlemen go in the back with Madam.'

'Good Lord, she must be the chauffeur!' Helen whispered as she and Sally went forward.

There was no doubt about it. When the two girls were seated one on each side of the old lady on the roomy cushioned seat, and Alec and Trevor were facing them on two seats that let down from the padded panel which divided the front of the old car from the back, Martin, looking more like a man than ever in her severe suit and hard hat, took the wheel with Colin at her side.

Mrs Pentland leaned across Helen and detached a speaking tube from its clip against the window.

'Very well, Martin,' she said and a moment later the car—which Colin said later must have been thirty years old if it was a day—passed majestically down the winding drive to the road.

8

Christmas Presents

The car reached the main road without mishap. Here, earlier traffic had cleared the surface and in five minutes or so the grey stone tower of a little church was showing through the leafless trees.

Darkling was little more than a hamlet huddled about the church. Martin, taking the big car alongside the churchyard wall, drew up outside a small door and jumped down to help her mistress from the back seat.

'This must be the stage door,' Helen whispered to Sally.

The old lady must have had very acute hearing for she glanced back at Helen.

'It happens to be the vestry door which the Rector and the choir use,' she said sharply. 'Follow me, if you please!'

Alec and Trevor grinned at the discomfited Helen, though Sally saw Colin Brent's mouth tighten for a moment. After what she had heard last night she supposed he was angry with Helen for antagonising the old lady. After all, they were all on trial and a little thing like this might spoil Helen's chances of coming in for the old lady's money.

The little church was half full and there was a great deal of craning forward and whispering as the Monk's Hollow party took their places in two of the front pews. Mrs Pentland, Martin, Helen and Trevor occupied one pew while Sally sat between Alec and Colin immediately behind.

Sally looked round appreciatively. The little stone church had been decorated with masses of holly and a lighted Christmas tree stood at the foot of the chancel steps. Flowers had been tastefully arranged on the altar and a lighted crib had been placed under one of the stained glass windows.

Sally felt tears prick into her eyes. Every Christmas since she was a child she had accompanied her father to church. Since his death her sense of loss had been so great that she had not attended services in London at Christmas time.

Just for a moment she sat with closed eyes, trying to imagine that it was her father sitting next to her now. She felt a gentle pressure on her arm and turned to find herself looking into Alec's kindly face as he smiled down at her. She smiled back at him. He too had suffered a big loss when his mother had died. Perhaps he was missing her as much as she was missing her own father.

The white surpliced choir, followed by the old Rector, came in procession from the vestry singing a Christmas hymn. Sally noticed that while Aunt Agatha joined in the singing the grim-faced woman by her side stared straight ahead, her lips unmoving. It was obvious that Martin was only in church as a matter of duty.

Sally found herself speculating about her great-aunt's attendant. Surely the old lady could have chosen someone a little more human to be her constant companion.

When the service was over Martin drove them all back to Monk's Hollow. Here a roaring fire in the open grate in the hall greeted them. The Christmas tree glowed at the foot of the stairs. For the first time Sally noticed that a big bunch of mistletoe was hanging from the overhead light in the centre of the hall.

As the old lady on Martin's arm went towards the stairs Colin hurried forward.

Before the astonished Mrs Pentland could do more than gasp he had given her a kiss.

'Young man!'—she gasped, then a twinkle came into her frosty eyes as she saw him looking up at the mistletoe. 'Go on with you! I'm much too old for that sort of thing.'

'No woman's ever too old to be kissed,' Colin laughed, and, chuckling, the old lady, leaning heavily on Martin's arm, started up the stairs.

Colin, a gleam in his eye, stationed himself beneath the mistletoe under which both Sally and Helen would have to pass if they wanted to go up to their rooms.

'Scared?' Colin grinned, seeing that they were both holding back.

'We're not scared at all, are we, Sally?' Helen asked, and putting her hand between Sally's shoulder blades, she propelled her sharply forward so that she found herself in Colin's arms. The resourceful Helen, laughing, ran past and was half-way up the stairs before Colin had kissed Sally.

'I'll get you later!' he cried after her, then looking down at Sally with a twinkle: 'But you left a very worthwhile substitute behind you. How about another for good measure, Sally?'

Sally felt his lips close over hers. He kissed with practised ease, and, when he showed no sign of releasing her, she pulled away from him. She noticed that Alec and Trevor had turned towards the sitting-room.

Conscious that her cheeks were flushed, she ran upstairs to her room. How silly she was to get so worked up about something as ordinary as a kiss under the mistletoe. Yet there had been something about Colin's manner which told her that he had wanted an opportunity of kissing her ever since he had come to the house and they had met.

When she had taken off her coat and changed her shoes she went downstairs again. The others were already in the sitting-room. Briggs was handing round sherry on a silver tray.

'The old lady's coming down to Christmas dinner which we're having at one o'clock,' Alec told her as she joined him by the fireplace.

'That'll put a damper on the merriment,' said Helen, who had overheard the remark.

'I don't see why you should say that!'

Trevor said sharply. 'After all, this is her house and she's doing her best to entertain us. This sherry, for instance, is excellent.'

'Hear, hear!' Colin cried, deftly replacing his empty glass on Brigg's tray and taking another full one. 'The way she let me kiss her under the mistletoe proves she's a good sport.'

'What sort of a present have you bought her, Sally?' Helen asked with a sly look out of her pale green eyes.

Sally's heart gave a lurch. She had had to leave London in such a hurry that she had not had time even to think about buying her Aunt Agatha a Christmas present. But she had no intention of letting Helen Renton know this.

'I think I'd rather keep it a secret if you don't mind, Helen,' she said.

'Just as you like,' Helen said with a little laugh. 'I don't mind people knowing that I've bought her a bottle of toilet water. I understand that old ladies use gallons of it in the year.'

'I got her some handkerchiefs,' Colin put in. 'I think she'll like them. The girl in the shop said they were hand embroidered.'

Alec, when pressed, admitted that he had bought the old lady a book.

'She used to write to my mother and say that one of her greatest joys in her old age was her love of reading,' he said. 'I only hope she likes my selection.'

Sally began to panic. Even Trevor, Helen's fiancé, had evidently bought her Aunt Agatha a gift. What would the old lady say if her only relative came to the Christmas dinner table empty handed! Then suddenly she had an inspiration. Before she had left her digs she had snatched up a framed snapshot of her father which she kept beside her bed. She had other photographs but this was her favourite and she had thought it would be nice to have it with her at Monk's Hollow.

When Briggs announced that dinner was ready she slipped upstairs. Just for a moment she stood with her father's picture in her hand. She thought the kindly eyes in the lined face were smiling approvingly at her as she moved to the dressing-table to take a piece of tissue-paper from one of the drawers.

Making the photograph into a neat little parcel she went downstairs again and joined the others as they crossed the hall to the dining-room.

The old lady was already seated at the end of the long table. As the young people seated themselves they saw that by the side of each plate was a little parcel. Colin was the first to open his. He gave a delighted whistle. 'Why, my dear Madam, what a lovely gift!' he cried. 'I don't deserve it.'

It was a slim leather wallet with gold corners. Mrs Pentland smiled.

'I hope you have some money to put in it,' she said and as Alec and Trevor opened their parcels and found identical wallets: 'And I hope you do too.'

Sally, removing the paper from the square parcel in front of her plate, saw that her gift was a lavishly equipped beauty case in green leather. Helen's was exactly the same except that it was in red.

As the two girls turned to thank her, Mrs Pentland said: 'I don't know that I approve of too much use of cosmetics for young girls, but I think that the care of the skin is all important.'

Colin rose to his feet and beamed round.

'I'm sure that the others will want me to say "Thank you" on their behalf, Madam,' he said. 'For my part, I am delighted with my present. I only wish that mine could have been a little more appropriate.'

He handed over the box of handkerchiefs and the old lady took it with a genuine look of pleasure.

'Why, my boy, I had no idea—' she began, but before she could say any more the others had placed their presents before her.

She opened them like an excited child. Sally, watching her, felt a stab of pity. Aunt Agatha might have plenty of money but it was obvious that she had missed most of the real pleasures of life. Receiving presents at Christmas, for instance.

At last all the little parcels were open, except one. Sally, with a fast beating heart, realised it was hers. She saw the old fingers pulling aside the tissue-paper, then looking down at the framed picture of the smiling man dressed in open-neck sports shirt and flannel trousers. The photograph had been taken on holiday and Sally, sitting there, had a sudden vision of her father standing being photographed by her with the hot sun pouring down on them and the sound of breaking waves on the beach behind her.

For some time the old lady did not speak. Sally began to wonder if she was annoyed. After all, she and her father had had a bitter quarrel which had never been made up. Last night she had seemed to regret that, but—well, one could never tell with old people.

Then she saw a tear roll down the lined old cheek.

Why, she's crying, she thought, and at that moment, her aunt raised her eyes and looked down the table towards her.

'It was a very kind gesture to give me this photograph of your father, Sally,' the old voice, trembling with emotion, said. 'I appreciate it very much. The only other photograph I have is of your father when he was little more than a child.'

Sally did not know what to say to this. To her relief the door opened at that moment and Briggs and the maid came into the room to serve the first course.

It was a merry meal. The highlight was the enormous turkey which Briggs and the maid carried into the room and placed on the sideboard.

'Who's going to carve?' Aunt Agatha demanded, looking first at Colin, then at Trevor and finally at Alec.

For a moment or two no one spoke and Briggs, with a sigh of resignation, picked up the carving knife and fork as if, all along, he had expected he would have to do the work.

Then Alec jumped up. 'I'll carve, if you like,' he said and his long legs carried him quickly to the sideboard, where the old servant gladly handed over the carving knife. Sally, watching the movement of his powerful shoulders as he bent intently over the turkey, thought what a nice man he was. Somehow she couldn't imagine either Colin or Trevor taking on such a job, but it was just the sort of thing Alec would do well. She could just imagine him in his own home carving for a big family of children.

She bit her lip at this thought. Somehow, for no reason at all, she preferred not to think of Alec as being married. She preferred him to be single.

What a silly fool I am! she chided herself, then fell to with a real appetite on the luscious plateful that had just been put in front of her.

After the meal there were crackers with the nuts and fruit, and then a return to the sitting-room for the coffee. Everybody was happy and at ease. Even Aunt Agatha laughed and talked as she could not have laughed and talked, Sally decided, for years. Just occasionally she would look down at the framed snapshot in her lap, and then she would smile at Sally so gratefully that Sally felt the sacrifice in giving up her father's photograph had been well worth while. In any case, she had other snapshots in her digs which she could frame to take the place of this one.

At half-past two Martin appeared to take Mrs Pentland to her room for her rest. When the old lady had gone Colin looked round.

'I've counted at least six yawns in the last two minutes,' he exclaimed. 'I suppose it's no good asking for a volunteer to go with me to bring my car up to the house. I don't want to leave it marooned in the snow for another night.'

Helen stretched her arms above her head and said she was going to sleep the heavy meal off. As neither Trevor nor Alec showed any enthusiasm for a tramp in the snow Sally smiled across at Colin.

'I'll come with you, Colin,' she said.

His face lit up. 'Right! I'll see you down in the hall in ten minutes. I don't think it will be too bad underfoot. There hasn't been any snow since last night.'

9

A Pirate in Modern Dress?

The sun shining from an eggshell blue sky turned the snowy landscape into a white wonderland as Sally and Colin started off down the drive to the road.

Colin, wearing a cap and a heavy belted overcoat over his tweeds, looked every inch a country gentleman. Sally told him this and he laughed.

'So I don't look like an actor, eh?' he said, looking down at her, and for once his eyes were serious. 'I must admit I don't feel like one today. Life would be much simpler if everyone lived in an old country house like Monk's Hollow, miles from anywhere.'

Sally laughed. 'Why, you'd be the first to miss London if you knew you were never to see it again.'

For a moment he hesitated, then he gave a short laugh. 'I suppose you're right, Sally, but—well, life can get very complicated at times.'

She wondered if something was worrying him, something back in London which he would have to face when his visit to Monk's Hollow was over. Perhaps he was in debt, perhaps some stagestruck girl was making a nuisance of herself. As they walked along he looked down at Sally curiously.

'Your aunt's a strange woman,' he said. 'I find it hard to make her out. At one moment she is charm itself, the next she acts as if she's made of iron. What do you think of her?'

'I hardly know her.' Sally replied. 'I only met her for the first time last night.'

'That's what seems so strange to me. You're her only relative and yet, for twenty years, she's ignored your existence. I just can't understand it.'

Sally, staring straight ahead, said a little bitterly: 'It's easy enough to understand if you know the story. My father was brought up by Aunt Agatha. She thought he would go into her husband's business and marry a girl of her choice. But he was independent. He chose the job he wanted to do and married—my mother. He and Aunt Agatha quarrelled bitterly and never spoke to each other again.'

'And your father is—dead?'

She nodded. 'Yes, he died just over two years ago. I suppose you're wondering why my great-aunt didn't get in touch with me when she knew my father was dead. Well, I wondered the same thing until last night, when she told me that she was out of the country when the solicitor wrote to her. When she tried to get in touch with me I had disappeared. I wanted to start a new life and, of course, I made no attempt to get in touch with her.'

'How did she find you in the end?'

'She employed enquiry agents. It took them quite a long time to track me down and by that time my great-aunt was out of the country again. When she returned she invited me here for Christmas.'

They had reached the main road now and turned right, away from the direction they had taken that morning when going to church. As they plodded along through the snow Colin said rather indignantly:

'I think it's most unfair of your aunt even to consider leaving her money to anyone other than her only relative!'

Sally shook her head. 'I don't see why she shouldn't do as she likes. After all, the money's hers.'

'I've a good mind to tell her that I shan't accept the money even supposing she's going to leave it to me,' Colin declared. 'I should never be able to enjoy a penny of it if I knew that you'd been left out of the will, Sally.'

Suddenly she remembered his voice as he had talked to Helen in the corridor outside her room last night. 'We must be sensible about the old girl's money, Helen,' he had said. 'It would be better to work together than against each other.'

That could only mean one thing. This man by her side meant, by hook or by crook, to get his hands on Aunt Agatha's money. If she hadn't heard him talking to Helen last night she might have been touched by his solicitude. Now she knew him for what he was: someone who was after the main chance.

He had probably convinced Helen that it was to her advantage to work with him so that, if Aunt Agatha left the money to Helen, he would ask her to marry him and share her good fortune with him.

Now he was trying to ingratiate himself with her, Aunt Agatha's only relative, hoping she too would fall for him—as Helen obviously must have done, and agree to marry him once he knew for certain the money was coming to her.

He was covering all possibilities. His only real danger, he must know, was Alec whom he could not influence.

Suddenly she felt afraid. If he thought he had Helen and her in his pocket what mightn't he do to Alec if it became obvious that the old lady was going to pick the young New Zealander as her heir?

Sally stole a glance at the man striding along by her side. He did not look the vicious type. Surely he would not do anything to harm Alec just because of the money.

Yet—yet how could she be sure? She must keep her eyes and ears open in the next few days and warn Alec if she felt he was in danger of any sort.

'There's the car!' Colin said suddenly, and Sally saw, at the roadside, a little red car against which the snow had drifted.

'Do you think you'll be able to move it?' Sally asked doubtfully as they approached.

He shrugged. 'It depends if the engine will start. I didn't break down last night, it was just that it was so dark I went off the road into a drift. My lights weren't very good and I decided I'd be safer walking the rest of the way.'

He opened the door and got behind the steering wheel. Switching on he pressed the self-starter. There was a feeble whirr but the engine did not start. With a sigh he climbed out and went round to the boot at the back from which he took the starting handle.

'I'll have to do it the hard way,' he said with a grin at Sally.

After cranking for several minutes the engine gave a feeble splutter and started. Colin scrambled behind the steering wheel again and revved up the engine.

'Now for it!' he said. 'Stand well clear, Sally.' A few seconds later, like an animal emerging from its lair, the little car edged forward pushing the drift aside as it did so.

'Hop in!' Colin said and Sally, going round the back of the car, slid into the seat by his side. With a great deal of spluttering and an occasional explosion from the exhaust, the car proceeded down the road in the direction of Monk's Hollow. Once, as they took a corner rather faster than was wise, the little car skidded on the icy surface and Sally gave a little gasp of fear. Colin, correcting the skid skilfully, grinned as he changed gear.

'Sorry I scared you, Sally,' he said. 'You're driving with dangerous Dan Mc-Grew now.'

Glancing at him she could tell he was enjoying himself thoroughly. To be at all interesting, life had to have an edge of danger or uncertainty. Perhaps that was why he was savouring the present situation at Monk's Hollow, where, determined to have Aunt Agatha's money, he was laying outrageous plans to make sure that he got it.

Suddenly she realised that, scoundrel though he was, she couldn't help but like him. He had a quality which no woman was able to resist: a dare-devil approach to life which scorned safety and convention.

He's a pirate in modern dress, she thought, and a sudden vision of Colin in a three-cornered hat with a cutlass in his hand so tickled her imagination that she chuckled.

'What's amusing you?' he wanted to know turning the car up the steep drive which led under the snow-covered trees to Monk's Hollow.

'Oh, nothing,' she said quickly, and

though he frowned at her as if angry that she would not confide in him, she said no more.

He parked the car outside the house and they went into the hall together. Colin, taking off his cap and coat, turned towards the sitting-room.

'I wonder if there's a cup of tea going,' he said. 'That champagne we had with the meal has made me thirsty.'

'I'll just go up to my room,' Sally said, 'I'll see you later.'

The house was very quiet. As she climbed the stairs she supposed that everybody must still be sleeping off the heavy midday meal. She glanced at her watch. It was nearly four o'clock. The others would probably be putting in an appearance at any moment now.

Outside the door of her room she paused. She thought she had heard movement at the other side. Remembering her alarming experience during the night she hesitated, not knowing whether to go into the room or find someone to go in with her.

Then she told herself not to be a nervous fool. She had probably imagined she had heard something. She listened intently and, as there was no other sound, she grasped the handle firmly and pushed the door open.

Then she gasped, seeing the man standing with his back to her at the far side of the room.

The mirror was no longer flush against the wall. It had swung back to reveal the dark passage behind.

As if conscious that he was being watched, the man turned slowly and looked across at Sally.

It was Alec Carpenter!

10

The Secret Passage

'Come in and shut the door, Sally!'

There was an urgent note in Alec's voice. Sally, not quite certain what she ought to do, nevertheless went into the room and pushed the door to behind her.

'What are you doing in my room?' she demanded, frowning across at him.

'That's soon explained!' For a moment he looked at the entrance to the secret passage. 'I realised last night that it was something more than a nightmare that had upset you. You're too sensible a girl, Sally, for a dream to send you running in a panic from your room in the middle of the night. As I lay thinking things over this afternoon I wondered if perhaps someone had got into your room and frightened you. It seemed unlikely that they had got in by way of the window or the door so—well, I decided to come in and look round. I found—this!'

Once more he looked at the entrance to the passage. Sally crossed to his side and peered into the dark opening.

'You're quite right, Alec,' she said in a low voice. 'Someone did come into the room last night. I suppose their intention was to frighten me.'

She shuddered and told him how the intruder's cold fingers had passed over her face before whoever it was had withdrawn to the passage and closed the mirror door behind them.

'It was pretty plucky of you to go on sleeping in the room after that happened,' Alec said, admiration in his voice. 'Most girls would have roused the house and demanded another room.'

'I didn't think I'd be troubled again,' Sally said. 'Before I went to sleep I felt round the frame of the mirror and discovered a button at the top. When I pressed it—'

'I found the same button,' Alec said quickly. 'The point is, what do you mean to do now?'

Sally hesitated, then suddenly made up her mind.

'I'm going to see where the passage goes to,' she said, and his eyes lit up.

'I hoped you'd say that,' he said. 'Any objection if I come with you?'

She shook her head. 'I'll be disappointed if you don't,' she declared. 'Have you a torch?'

'In my room. I'll go and fetch it.'

He was soon back. He glanced at Sally. 'Shall I lead the way?' he asked, and when she nodded, he stepped into the cold dankness of the narrow passage.

Sally kept a few feet behind him as, cautiously, he moved slowly forward. After a few feet the passage turned abruptly to the left. The beam of the powerful torch fell on rough stone walls dripping with moisture. The ceiling was low, and, though Sally could manage by bending her head forward, Alec, who was much taller, was forced to crouch almost double as he shuffled his way forward.

'There don't seem to be any doors or passages opening off the main one,' he said over his shoulder to Sally. 'We'd best just go forward and see where we come out.'

Half a minute later the passage ended abruptly with a blank wall. Alec shone the torch on it, then looked at Sally, puzzled, as she stood just behind him.

'There doesn't seem to be any exit here,' he muttered, 'yet whoever came to your room, must have got into the passage by some entrance.'

'Shall I look on the wall on this side and you look on the other?' Sally suggested.

'All right,' he agreed. 'Here! You take the torch and I'll use my cigarette lighter.'

Sally shone the beam on the wall at her side. There was little to see but the wet mouldy stones with which the wall had been constructed. But she ran her fingers along the crevices hoping to find some hidden protuberance similar to the one she had discovered over the mirror in her bedroom.

But she had no success. Presently she

turned to Alec who shook his head dolefully.

'I'm afraid there's nothing doing, Sally,' he said. 'I've explored every crack and pressed every rough piece of stone. We'll just have to go back to your room.'

He moved a trifle impatiently and Sally, because the passage was narrow, had to move back rather abruptly. Her foot came down heavily in the corner formed by the end wall and the wall she had explored so thoroughly with the torch. There was a sudden click and a gasp from Alec.

'It's opening,' he said excitedly.

Slowly a section of the wall slid aside. Alec, who was holding the torch again, shone its beam on the damp flagstones at their feet.

'It must be operated when you stand on that stone in the corner,' he said. 'It's only with you moving to get out of my way that you stood on it. Good for you, Sally!'

He shone the torch through the opening. A few yards beyond the end of the wall was a wooden door. He took a cautious step or two forward and looked round.

'I seem to be inside a cupboard,' he said, and Sally, standing beside him, noticed that there were brooms and mops propped in one corner and a couple of buckets on the floor.

'It looks like a cupboard for cleaning utensils,' she said. 'Shall we open the door and look out?'

'Just a minute!' Alec put his ear to the door and listened. 'I don't think there's anybody about. Here goes!'

Cautiously he turned the handle and slowly opened the door. They found themselves looking out into a lighted passage. A little further along was a window beyond which could be seen the darkening sky of the winter afternoon.

'I've been along this passage before,' Sally said with a little frown. Then she looked at Alec quickly. 'Do you remember that last night I told you that I'd seen a weeping woman who appeared to be wearing a cowl?' He nodded. She hurried on: 'It was just a little further along. I told you, after she had disappeared, that I went to see where she had gone. There was a narrow staircase leading up into the darkness, though I did not explore it. I was scared and went back to the main part of the house.'

Alec closed the cupboard door. 'We might as well go and look for your staircase

110

now,' he said. She followed him and, after a few feet, he exclaimed: 'Is this it?' Sally, excitement rising in her, nodded.

'Yes, that's it! Shall we go up and look where it goes to?'

Directing the torch's beam up the narrow flight Alec led the way, with Sally a few inches behind. Suddenly he came to an abrupt halt so that she almost cannoned into him.

'What is it, Alec?' she whispered. He stepped aside so that she could see the object on which he had focused the torch. The short flight of steps ended abruptly. A door barred their way.

'I'm going to see if it's open,' Alec muttered. 'In for a penny, in for a pound.'

Sally held her breath as he put out his hand and turned the knob. He applied pressure but the door did not open. He looked back at her and shook his head.

'Whoever your weeping ghost was,' he declared, 'she must have had a key. This door's locked!'

'What do we do now?' Sally asked.

'Go back to your room via the secret passage,' he replied. 'It would be best if we closed the wall leading out of the cupboard behind us and the mirror door which lets into your room. No one knows we've found them yet. It might be as well to keep the whole thing secret for the time being.'

They passed through the opening which Alec closed by pressing on the stone Sally had discovered earlier. A couple of minutes later they were back in Sally's bedroom with the mirror door in place once more. Alec eyed the massive dressing-table.

'I think between us we should be able to move that rather formidable piece of furniture across the mirror,' he said. 'That will effectively stop anyone getting into your room in the night again.'

'But isn't the maid going to be puzzled when she sees that the dressing-table's been moved?' Sally exclaimed.

Alec shrugged. 'Oh, just say that you couldn't see very well when you were doing your hair and called me in to help you move the dressing-table nearer the window.'

Sally smiled a trifle doubtfully. 'I suppose that's a fairly convincing explanation,' she said, but already he was standing at the end of the dressing-table bracing himself to push the heavy piece of furniture across the six feet or so which divided it from the mirror. There was nothing else for it and Sally went forward to help him.

11

A Cowardly Assault

When Alec and Sally went down to the sitting-room they found Colin sitting eating hot buttered toast at a small table before the fire. He looked round with a smile when they appeared.

'Am I glad to see you!' he cried. 'I've been sitting here in solitary state for the best part of half an hour. Where is everybody?'

'I've been resting,' Alec said. 'All that roast turkey took some digesting, I can tell you.'

Colin grinned. 'Have some hot buttered toast!'

At Alec's grimace he got up and crossed to the bell push. 'I'll ring for some fresh tea. This has been made about half an hour.'

When the door opened, however, it was not Briggs who entered but Trevor Carley. The young man's good-looking face was tense with worry.

'Hello, what's up with you?' Colin cried.

'I can't find Helen,' Trevor exclaimed distractedly. 'I've just been to her room and—it's empty. I—I'm afraid something might have happened to her.' Alec took the other's arm and drew him towards the fire.

'What could have happened to her?' he asked quietly. 'Perhaps she's gone out for a walk.'

'But it's dark now and—besides—' Trevor broke off as if not knowing how to go on and say what was in his mind.

'Besides—what?' Sally asked.

He began to walk agitatedly up and down the room. 'I may as well tell you. After dinner, when we went upstairs, Helen and I had a terrible row. I won't tell you what it was about. That doesn't matter. But finally she flung off and went to her room and I went to mine. I was very angry at the time but, when I had calmed down, I decided to go and apologise to her. I knocked on the door but she did not reply. I thought she must be resting

114

and I decided to go back later. Well, I've just been back and when I still didn't get a reply I opened the door and looked in and she wasn't there.'

Briggs came in with fresh tea at this moment. Sally poured a cup and handed it to Trevor.

'You'll feel better after a cup of tea,' she told him. 'I'm sure Helen will walk in at any moment. You've no real reason for thinking any harm might have come to her, have you?'

'It's—it's just something she said,' he muttered, looking from one intent face to the other.

'What was that?' Alec asked.

Trevor drew a deep breath. 'She said she felt there was something strange about this house, almost as if someone was watching all the time. She said it gave her the shivers. When we quarrelled she said she wished she was back in London.'

Colin laughed. 'I'm sure you're letting your imagination run away with you, Trevor,' he cried. 'Helen strikes me as being a very sensible sort of girl. She's not the hysterical type, I'm sure.'

'That's just the point.' Trevor looked at him with dislike. It flashed across Sally's mind that perhaps the row between him and Helen had been about—Colin.

'What do you want us to do then?' Alec asked.

Trevor frowned. 'I'm not quite sure. Perhaps the best thing we could do first is to look in the grounds. If she's had an accident she might be lying out there now. If she's not found she might freeze to death.'

'Then we'd better go and get our coats on,' Alec said, and turned towards the door.

Colin gave an exaggerated sigh, finished his cup of tea and followed Alec.

As he passed Trevor he said:

'You're quite sure she's not having a bath, aren't you? It's quite possible, you know.'

Sally, who was looking at Trevor, saw the glare of hate which came into his eyes as they followed Colin's broad back as they left the room. Not for the first time she felt an ominous sense of impending disaster, as if events were building up to a climax which would affect them all.

'Hadn't you better get your coat on as well, Trevor?' she asked when he did not move. 'You'll want to go with Alec and Colin, won't you?'

He started, as if he had forgotten she was there.

'Yes, of course,' he muttered and went from the room.

Sally hesitated. She was not sure whether the men would want her with them when they were searching the grounds, yet she felt she could not remain inactive in the house while the search was in progress. In any case, there was a lot of ground to be covered round Monk's Hollow and every pair of eyes would be needed to penetrate the darkness looking for Helen's tracks in the snow.

Suddenly making up her mind she went from the room and ran up the stairs to get her coat. She tied a warm woollen scarf over her hair, then went back to the hall again. Alec and Colin were already there and Trevor appeared a few seconds later.

As they left the house they saw with dismay that snow was falling heavily again. Alec, looking up into the dark sky, said:

'I wonder how long it's been snowing?'

'It was just beginning when Sally and I came back to the house nearly an hour ago,' Colin said. 'I noticed the first few flakes as I got out of the car.'

'Then if it's been falling as heavily as this for nearly an hour there won't be many footprints to guide us,' Alec said glumly, and Sally, looking at the space in front of the house where Trevor's and Colin's cars were parked, saw that even the tracks of the tyres had been almost obliterated.

However, Alec said they had better cast around in case any of Helen's footsteps showed. They went along the edge of the lawn and walked for some distance down the drive. But there was no sign of any footprints.

'There's only one thing to do,' Alec said, looking round. 'We'll have to split up and search a part of the grounds singly. Colin, you go into the trees to the left of the drive, and you take the right hand side, Trevor. Sally and I will go to the other side of the house and look there.'

As the two young men disappeared into the trees Alec took Sally's arm in a firm grip. As she looked up into his serious face she asked quietly:

'Do you really think that Helen is out there, lying helpless somewhere in the snow, Alec?'

He shrugged. 'If Trevor assures us she's not in the house she must be outside it, mustn't she?' he said slowly.

But somehow, from the tone of his voice, she could not help but feel that he had little faith in the search.

Sally was surprised, as they groped their way by the light of Alec's torch, through the blinding snowstorm, at the extent of her aunt's property. Though Monk's Hollow looked a sizeable house viewed from the front, the back quarters and outbuildings seemed to stretch interminably into the darkness.

Alec must have had the same thought as her, for suddenly he said: 'No wonder the old place is honeycombed with secret passages. Your aunt must have dozens of rooms she hasn't any use for. I don't suppose she's ever been in half of them.'

They came to a group of buildings on their left which had obviously at some time been stables, though they were now shuttered and deserted. Beyond the snow was driven by a bitter wind across what must have been open fields, though there was little to see in the intense darkness.

'It would be like looking for a needle in a haystack to go out there,' Alec said, shielding his eyes with his hands from the driving snow as he peered into the black void ahead. 'In any case, Helen isn't likely to have come this way for a walk, I'm sure. I think we'd better join the others—'

'What's that?'

Sally thought she had heard a feeble cry from somewhere near at hand. Startled, she looked up at Alec. His tense face told her that he too had heard it.

'We'd better take a look round,' he muttered and strode past Sally to the nearest door at the end of the stables. But it was locked and resisted all his efforts to open it. With Sally a few feet behind, he walked the length of the building. Turning a corner he found another door. He gave a sudden exclamation, which brought Sally hurrying to his side.

'What is it?' she demanded.

He nodded at the ground at his feet. The wind was blowing the falling flakes past the sheltered corner where they stood. Clearly in the snow at their feet were footprints leading into the building. Suddenly Alec gave the door a violent push and it flew back against the wall.

'I'm going in,' he said and stepped forward, the beam of his torch probing into the darkness beyond.

Sally followed, her heart thundering. What would they find in the dark building?

She looked round and saw that they were in a long room with stalls for half a dozen horses. They had obviously not been used for a long time for there was an air of neglect, even of decay, about the whole place.

Alec went slowly forward but his pace quickened when again he heard a feeble cry from the far end.

'Here she is!' he called over his shoulder, and went down on one knee beside the crumpled figure of the girl lying there.

Sally, hurrying to his side, saw him raise Helen and cradle her fair head on his arm. Helen's eyes were open and she looked up into Alec's face in a bewildered way.

'Oh, I'm so glad you've come,' she sobbed. 'I seem to have been lying here for hours.'

'We'll soon get you back to the house,' he said gently. 'Do you think you can stand up?'

'I feel dizzy when I stand,' she said in a complaining voice. 'Someone hit me over the head and I must have been unconscious for some time. But—but—if you'll help me I'll try to stand.'

With Alec on one side and Sally on the other they walked her down the length of the stable to the door. But there she began to sag down again and Alec, with a quick glance at Sally, said:

'I'd better carry her. You hold the torch, Sally.'

He gathered Helen up into his arms and they went out into the snow again. Soon they were walking alongside the big sprawling bulk of the old house back to the front door.

'I'll take her in while you call for the others, Sally,' Alec said. 'They should be coming in at any time now, in any case. We agreed to meet in twenty minutes if Helen wasn't found.'

Sally went to the top of the drive and called Colin's and Trevor's names. Colin was the first to appear.

'Have you found her?' he cried, but before she could reply Trevor appeared through the trees. She told them both what had happened and they all went into the house. Alec had laid Helen before the fire and had poured some brandy into a glass which he was putting to her lips. Trevor ran forward and went on one knee by her side.

'Helen, darling, what happened? Sally says someone knocked you out.'

Helen nodded. 'I'm lucky to be alive,' she whispered.

'But what possessed you to go plunging out into the snow like that?' Trevor demanded, and, at the look on her face, 'Oh, I'm sorry for what I said. I didn't mean half of it.'

'You should have thought of that before you said all those things,' she said querulously. 'I thought I wasn't wanted—so I decided—'

'Helen, honey, I love you,' Trevor said distractedly. 'If I'd known you were going to do a thing like this I—I'd never have said a word.'

'What did happen, Helen?' Colin asked curiously. 'Who could have hit you over the head?'

She looked at him exasperatedly. 'If I knew that I'd call in the police!' she said sharply. 'All I know is that I decided, as it was snowing, not to venture far from the house and I thought I'd explore the outbuildings. I suppose whoever followed me must have been able to come right up behind me without being heard because of the snow. All I know is that I heard a sudden movement, then, when I turned, something came down on my head and I remember nothing more until I came to in that stable. Every time I tried to get up I went dizzy and fell down again. Then—then Alec and Sally came.'

'Thank God they found you,' Trevor said fervently. 'Now I'd better get a doctor to you.'

But she shook hear head, with a grimace of pain as she did so.

'I don't want a doctor!' she declared. 'Stop fussing, Trevor. In any case, no doctor's going to get out here this evening in this snowstorm.'

Sally was the first to notice that the door was open and that Martin, her great-aunt's companion was standing there. Meeting Sally's eyes she smiled frostily.

'Perhaps I might be of assistance in finding out whether Miss Renton needs the doctor or not,' she said, coming forward. 'I am a fully qualified nurse.'

They stood aside as she bent over Helen and ran practised fingers over her skull. As she straightened, she looked round.

'I think Miss Renton has not suffered

any real damage,' she said in her precise way, 'though she may have a sore head for a few days.'

She looked round. 'I have a message for you from my mistress. She regrets she does not feel up to having supper with you but she hopes to join you in here for coffee afterwards.'

Without another word she turned on her heel and made for the door, but before she left the room she looked back.

'Do you intend to tell the police about this unfortunate happening, Miss Renton?' she asked.

'I think she should!' Trevor exclaimed. 'We can't let this bloke, whoever he is, get away with this. None of us will feel safe if he's left free to roam about—'

'Oh, shut up, Trevor!' Helen said heatedly. 'What do you think Mrs Pentland will say if we drag the police in? They'll tramp round in their big boots, asking us all questions. There'll be no peace for anybody for the rest of Christmas.'

'Well, I don't know,' Trevor said doubtfully, but Helen, looking across at the woman standing in the doorway, said: 'I don't think you need tell your mistress. It would only upset her.'

Sally, watching Martin's face, seemed to see a flicker of relief cross its grim features.

'Very well, miss,' she said and, turning away, she went from the room, closing the door behind her.

12

Ghost Story

Supper that evening was a subdued meal. Only Sally and the three young men sat at the end of the long table in the dining-room. Helen was resting in her room. Mrs Pentland had sent another message by Martin to say that, though she was having her meal sent upstairs, she would join the party in the sitting-room later.

Sally noticed that Trevor had very little to say. Colin, on the other hand, kept up a constant flow of small talk. Once Sally saw Trevor look up from his plate and glance at Colin. And she drew a sharp breath as she saw, for a moment, the look of dislike which came into his eyes. It was obvious

126

that he blamed the actor for the bad feeling that now existed between himself and the girl he loved.

Alec for once had little to say, though he smiled dutifully from time to time at Colin's gay quips, even entered into a mild argument with him about modern jazz music.

But everybody was relieved when the meal was over and they could go to the sitting-room for coffee. As they crossed the hall Colin said:

'I wonder what time the old girl will put in an appearance?'

They glanced up the wide staircase but it was Helen, still looking white and shaken, who was coming towards them.

'Why, darling, should you be up?' Trevor cried in some consternation hurrying forward.

But she brushed past his outstretched hand and smiled at Colin.

'That quiet room began to get on my nerves,' she said. 'I couldn't stick it any longer.'

'Do you feel fit to be out of bed?' Alec asked.

She nodded and the light from the overhead light trembled in her spun gold hair.

'I'm all right,' she said. 'I can rest as easily down here as up there by myself.'

'I would have sat with you,' Trevor put in but again she ignored him.

'Shall we go into the sitting-room?' she suggested. 'It's cold out here.'

They followed her as she turned away, though Sally noticed Alec's glance at the log fire in the open grate as if puzzled how anyone could complain of the cold with such a blaze to warm them.

Helen opened the sitting-room door then halted on the threshold.

'Good evening, Mrs Pentland!' she said and there was just enough of surprise in her voice to tell Sally that she hadn't expected to find the old lady established by the fireside.

'Come in and close the door!' the old lady cried.

As they went forward she went on: 'I hear from Briggs that you had an accident this afternoon.'

Helen frowned. 'I was hoping you wouldn't hear,' she muttered.

'But why not, my dear? I like to know what goes on in my own house, you know.'

'Yes, I know, but—well, I didn't want you to be worried–'

'What exactly did happen?' The old lady's voice was sharper now.

'Someone hit her over the head and left her lying in one of the stables at the back of the house,' Trevor put in quickly and earned himself a glare from Helen. 'She might have frozen to death.'

Mrs Pentland looked round. Her face was shocked.

'But who would do such a thing?'

Before anyone could reply to this question the door opened and Martin appeared. She was carrying a shawl. Crossing to her mistress's side she placed this about her shoulders.

'Did you know about Miss Renton's—accident this afternoon, Martin?' she asked.

'Yes, Madam. I would have told you but—well, Miss Renton asked me not to. She didn't want you to worry.'

'But she should have seen a doctor, the police, too.'

'I examined her head myself, Madam. In my view the bruise was quite superficial. As for the police—'

'But I can't have my guests assaulted

129

like this!' the old lady cried. 'Get on to the local constable in Darkling, Martin, at once.'

'Oh, please don't!' Helen pleaded. 'It can do no good now. After all, as Martin says, I've not been badly hurt.'

'Well, just as you like,' Mrs Pentland said doubtfully, then waved her companion away. 'That will be all, Martin. I'll ring when I want you.'

'Yes, Madam,' the woman said and turned to the door.

As she passed Sally noticed that her lips were set in a grim line and that there was a faint flush on her pale cheeks. She doesn't like being treated like a servant, that's obvious, Sally thought, then looked back at Aunt Agatha as the old lady spoke again.

'As Helen seems to be none the worse for her unhappy experience you'd better all sit down and make yourselves comfortable,' she said. 'Alec, my dear, ring the bell and Briggs will bring coffee. While you drink it we'll decide how to entertain ourselves on this important occasion. After all, it is Christmas night.'

Alec suggested songs round the piano but when it was found that no one could play the lovely baby grand in the corner the suggestion was dropped.

It was Colin who proposed charades. The old lady nodded.

'I haven't seen charades played since I was a child,' she cried. 'Pick your team, Colin.'

'There are hardly enough of us for two teams,' he said. 'As Helen's not feeling too fit, why don't the rest of us act a charade for your benefit and hers, Madam?'

'Very well! Off you go!'

Out in the hall Colin suggested 'supplication' as the word.

'Sup is easy,' he said. 'You, Alec, pretend to be in a pub quarrelling with Trevor and Sally. I'll come in as the village constable and tell you to be quiet. I'll work the word "sup" in easy enough.'

Trevor frowned. 'Can't you leave me out?' he muttered.

'Why, don't you feel well?' Colin asked but Sally could tell, from the scornful tone of his voice, that he was not at all concerned about Trevor's health.

'Come on, Trevor, it's just to please the old lady,' Alec said in a conciliatory voice.

Trevor forced a smile. 'OK,' he said but

he did not look at Colin as they moved toward the sitting-room door.

The second word, 'lick' was acted out in a village schoolroom. Alec was the schoolmaster who had to apply the cane to Colin.

Out in the hall Trevor muttered: 'How are you going to do the last syllable? It seems unfair to me to act it as "Asian".'

'Don't be so fussy!' Colin said and Trevor bit his lip. Perhaps, Sally thought, he was remembering that it wasn't many hours since Helen had said the same thing to him.

In spite of Trevor's protest they wrapped scarves round their heads and pretended to be Arabs.

For the acting of the whole word Sally had to be a beggar with a bowl begging alms from the passing crowd.

'Now then, how near did you come to guessing?' Colin asked when, having divested the coats and rugs they had used for dressing up, they returned to the sitting-room.

'It all seemed a great big muddle to me,' Helen said a trifle crossly.

'I think the first word was "sup" and the last, something to do with the Sheik of Araby,' Aunt Agatha declared, knitting her brow. 'But I can't make a word out of that.'

'We thought the second syllable was easy,' Alec put in encouragingly.

'You were obviously licking a small boy at school,' Helen yawned. 'Beyond that I haven't a clue.'

'Sup—lick—I've got it "supplication"!' the old lady cried triumphantly. 'Well done, Helen. You were very observant.'

'What shall we do now?' Colin asked. 'More charades?'

No one seemed very enthusiastic. Alec with a smile said:

'I've always wanted to hear a real English ghost story told in the right setting at Christmas time. Somehow it's not the same in New Zealand where the temperature's often in the nineties around Christmas time!'

'A good idea!' the old lady cried. 'Now, who's going to tell the story?'

Helen glanced at Colin. 'I'm sure Colin knows heaps of stories. All actors do!'

'Well?' Mrs Pentland asked, glancing across at the actor.

He shrugged and smiled. 'I know a few. I gave a recital once at Christmas.

If you like I'll tell you the horrible story of Toby Barley and how he lost his head on Christmas Eve.'

'Sit down all of you!' the old lady ordered. 'Alec, turn out the lights. Ghost stories are much better told in the firelight.'

'And I think we'd better have the curtains back as well,' Colin said, crossing to the window and swishing the heavy hangings back.

An anticipatory little shiver went down Sally's back as the cold light of the newly risen moon shone into the room. Outside the snow lay thick on the lawn and trees. It was an ideal setting for a ghost story, she decided, glancing at Colin who was now standing, back to the fire, looking round at his audience.

'The snow was falling heavily one Christmas Eve at the turn of the century,' he began in a low voice which yet carried to every corner of the big room. 'Toby Barley, leaving the village inn, took his horse from the stable, mounted and turned towards home...'

The story went on to tell how Toby, a prosperous farmer, lost his way in the blizzard and found himself riding up the driveway to a house all ablaze with lights. Toby, knocking on the door to ask the way, was invited in by a jolly man dressed in a costume of long ago. Toby was given food and drink and went into the big room which had been cleared for dancing. Here men and women in fancy dress were enjoying themselves to their heart's content.

Toby's glass was filled to the brim whenever he emptied it. Soon he began to feel sleepy. He wandered away and found an empty room with a fire and a comfortable sofa. Lying on this he fell asleep.

'When he wakened he found himself lying, shivering with cold, in the snow,' Colin said slowly. 'Around him were ruined walls and the empty sockets of glassless windows. He jumped up and stumbled out into the dawn. His horse, poor beast, was waiting for him. Leaping into the saddle he spurred the animal into a gallop and rode away from that accursed place which, he later discovered, had fallen into ruin many hundred of years before.'

Sally's imagination pictured the scene vividly as she listened. Her eyes were on the window as she looked out into the snowy moonlit garden. She could almost see the farmer lurching out of the ruined house, terror in his heart...

Suddenly she stiffened. Her breath left her body in a startled gasp.

For something had come to the window and was staring into the firelit room, a thin cowled figure which stood swaying there in the moonlight.

The tension was so great that Sally could not hold back the scream that rose in her throat.

'What is it, Sally?' Alec demanded, turning to her at his side.

'There, there, at the window!' she gasped, lying back in her seat, her hands over her eyes.

Trevor had run to switch the light on. Colin had made for the window.

'But there's nothing there, Sally!' he said, turning to look back at her.

'But I saw it!' she said, close to hysteria. 'It—it was the same cowled figure I saw in the corridor the night I came here.'

'Nonsense! You must have imagined it!' Aunt Agatha said sharply. 'Colin told his tale so convincingly that you would see a ghost in any shadow, Sally.'

'But—but I did see it,' she cried. 'I'm sure of it.'

'Well, if it was there it would leave footprints,' Trevor said. 'Let's go and look.'

Alec crossed to the window and opened it. He looked out then shook his head.

'There are no footprints,' he said, and Aunt Agatha sniffed.

'Shut the window, Alec,' she exclaimed. 'And pull the curtains. If you leave them open Sally's likely to see an elephant or something looking in at us!'

Everyone laughed at that except Sally whose heart was still pounding. She caught sight of Helen who was glancing at Colin as if pleased.

She's thinking that this is a black mark against me with Aunt Agatha, she thought. But I don't care. I did see something. I'm sure of it.

She glanced at Alec but he did not meet her eyes. With a sinking heart she wondered if he too believed she had let her imagination run away with her as she listened to Colin's ghost story.

Suddenly she wished she was back in London. Her digs were lonely enough but at least she could be herself there. She felt tears come smarting into her eyes and turned her head so that Trevor, who was looking curiously at her, would not see that she was crying.

13

Almost a Tragedy

The party broke up shortly after that. Sally, saying goodnight, slipped away while the others were grouped round the old lady as she waited for Martin to take her up to bed.

As she climbed the stairs Sally's thoughts were bitter. She knew that everybody thought her a silly scared little thing who had let her imagination run away with her. What a pity it was that only she had been looking towards the window when the apparition, or whatever it was, had stood there for a moment looking in. But everybody including Alec had been watching Colin as he brought his terrifying story to an end.

It was cold in the bedroom for the fire

had sunk into a few dying embers. Though there was coal in the box by the side of the grate Sally decided it was not worth while making the fire up again.

Hurrying, she slipped out of her clothes and into the big bed where, to her relief, she found a hot water bottle waiting for her. As she lay in the darkness, waiting for sleep to come, she made up her mind that she would leave Monk's Hollow on the following day without fail. There had been some talk about the party breaking up the next day, though Trevor for one had not been enthusiastic about the suggestion saying he was expected back the day after Boxing Day. Sally, too, knew that she was expected back at the office immediately after the holiday and did not want to risk losing her job for the sake of the extra day.

Now she felt she would like to be off in the morning and the earlier the better. She could not bear to think of staying an hour longer in this awful house than she need do.

'You'll not see Alec again,' a little voice seemed to whisper but she buried her face in the pillow as if to shut it out. In any case, she thought, Alec probably thought she was as big a fool as the others for making out she had seen a ghost when there was no ghost to be seen!

She tried to sleep, but sleep just would not come. She tossed and turned growing more and more frustrated as time passed.

Suddenly she sat up in the darkness. She knew she would not be able to rest properly until she had spoken to her aunt and told her she was leaving early in the morning.

She put on the light and looked at her watch. It was only midnight. She was amazed. She was quite sure she had been in bed for at least four or five hours.

She scrambled out of bed and pulled on a wrap. Perhaps her aunt would not yet be asleep. She would look into the room and, if the old lady was asleep, she would creep back to her own room. If Aunt Agatha was awake still she would say she was leaving immediately after breakfast and say good-bye there and then.

She opened her door. The corridor outside was silent in the light of the small lamp which glowed in the ceiling. She walked silently over the carpet towards her aunt's room, her heart thudding in her breast.

She wondered if Alec was asleep. Just for a moment her heart sank. If she slipped away early in the morning she would not even be able to say good-bye to him. What would he think of her? But perhaps he would not be concerned. After all, he had not given any sign of thinking she had become at all special in his life.

She crossed the landing at the top of the stairs and continued along the passage until she came to her aunt's door.

She put her ear to the panel and listened. There was no sound beyond the door though, as she stood there, a puzzled little frown came to her brow.

She could smell smoke!

She looked down at her feet and saw a little curl of smoke coming under the door.

A moment later she had turned the handle and thrown the door open.

A gust of thick oily smoke poured out at her. Groping her way forward into the dark room she made for the bed. Luckily she remembered its exact position from her previous visit to the room, though by the time she reached it she was coughing and choking as the smoke crept into her lungs.

She groped with outstretched arms and, to her relief, felt the soft warmth of the old lady's body. With a superhuman effort she pulled the bedclothes back and scooped up the pathetically tiny body and made for the door, feeling as if her lungs were bursting.

How she reached the corridor outside she never knew. But suddenly she was lying on something soft gulping the cool air into her straining lungs, her aunt's unconscious body beside her.

At last she raised herself. Though her head was spinning she managed, by supporting herself against the wall, to stand upright. She looked round. Smoke was still billowing from her aunt's room through the open door. She knew she must get help as quickly as possible before the fire took a firmer hold and threatened the whole house.

'Help!'

The sound came feebly from her parched throat. She tried again as she ran to the nearest door and hammered on it.

Trevor's startled face looked out at her.

'Good God, what's happened?' he demanded.

'My aunt's room—it's on fire,' Sally

mumbled, then as a wave of dizziness swept over her, she swayed and slipped to the floor again.

When she came round again she heard Alec's voice saying firmly:

'Now just lie still! You'll be all right in a minute or two.'

'But my aunt–?' she gasped trying to struggle up.

'She's been taken to another room. She's alive—thanks to you.'

Sally closed her eyes once more. When she opened them again she felt better and looked round. She had been placed on a couch which stood in a recess near the top of the stairs. There was a strong smell of smoke in the air. As she watched she saw Martin hurry past and go into a room near at hand. Evidently her aunt had been taken there now her own room was unusable because of the fire.

She sat up. Where was Alec? And Trevor and Colin?

She looked towards her aunt's room and saw the three young men emerge, with blackened hands and faces, into the corridor.

'Alec!' she called and he came quickly to her side. He smiled.

'Everything's under control!' he said. 'We tipped the burning mattress from the window and it's burned itself out in the snow.'

She frowned. 'Burning mattress? But do you mean that—?'

'I mean that it seems as if your great-aunt must have been smoking in bed,' he declared. 'Evidently she fell asleep and the smouldering cigarette set fire to the mattress. It was lucky you turned up when you did or she'd undoubtedly have been suffocated.'

Into Sally's mind came a clear picture of her interview with her aunt on the night of her arrival when she had gone to the old lady's bedroom and found her sitting up in bed. She had been smoking then.

She shivered suddenly realising that it had only been because she could not sleep that she had gone along to Aunt Agatha's room at all.

'How is she?' she asked, looking up into Alec's begrimed face.

'It's hard to say,' he replied. 'Martin's rung for the doctor and he's coming out at once. We'll know more when he's examined her.'

Colin now came forward and looked a

trifle anxiously down at Sally. Trevor stood in the background.

'How did you come to turn up outside the old girl's bedroom so conveniently?' Colin asked, and added hastily: 'It's a good thing you did. She'd have been a goner for sure if you hadn't paid her a visit just at that moment.'

'I couldn't sleep,' Sally said. 'I thought I'd go along and—'

She broke off. She couldn't very well blurt out that she had intended to tell her aunt she would be leaving in the morning.

She was saved from having to say more by the ringing of a bell.

'That must be the doctor,' Trevor said as Martin appeared and hurried towards the stairs.

Presently the doctor, a thin tall man with a serious face and the look of someone who had been unceremoniously dragged out of bed, came upstairs and made into the room where the old lady had been taken.

Colin lit a cigarette and glanced at Alec.

'I wonder if she'll pull through,' he muttered. 'She's pretty old to go through such an experience.'

'If she dies you won't have to worry about the will any more, will you?' Trevor asked, rather spitefully, Sally thought.

Colin's face darkened. 'It may surprise you to know that I wasn't thinking about the will. All I want is for the old girl to live.'

'Naturally,' Trevor murmured and turned and walked away as Colin, biting his lip, fist upraised, made a move towards him.

'That fellow loathes me,' Sally heard him mutter. 'Why does he think it's my fault that Helen prefers me to him?'

Sally wondered where Helen was. In bed, she supposed. Perhaps she had not heard the commotion caused by the fire. After her experience that afternoon she had probably taken something to make her sleep and had slept ever since she got into bed.

Presently the doctor came out of Mrs Pentland's room accompanied by Martin.

'She'll need watching carefully,' he said. 'I'll call again in the morning.'

Alec stepped forward. 'How is Mrs Pentland?' he asked.

The doctor hesitated before replying. 'She's had a nasty experience. Mrs Martin

146

here tells me she often smoked in bed. It is a dangerous habit, especially for one so old. However, thanks to the person who rescued her, she's likely to live. She breathed a fair amount of smoke in, but she seems to have pretty tough lungs. I think she'll come through.'

Sally was surprised at the surge of emotion she felt at these words. She had had no idea that she would feel so relieved at the news that her aunt was going to get better. Up to that moment she had looked upon Aunt Agatha as a rather tiresome old woman who had tried to bully her father and had failed. Now she saw her as a lonely, almost friendless old thing who, but for a lucky chance, would have died a cruel death.

'When can I see her?' she asked on impulse.

The doctor frowned. 'Who are you, my dear?'

'She saved Mrs Pentland's life,' Colin put in. 'She's the old lady's only relative.'

'I think you might go to her—but only for a couple of minutes, mind,' the doctor said, and added: 'What you did was very brave, my dear. Your aunt has reason to be grateful to you.'

Sally, feeling the colour rising in her cheeks at this praise, made for the door of her aunt's room. Martin accompanied her.

'She may be asleep,' she whispered as she followed Sally into the dark room where the only light came from a bedside lamp.

But the old lady, propped against her pillows, was awake. Feebly she said:

'Who is it?'

'It's your niece, Madam,' Martin replied. 'The doctor says she can see you for a few seconds.'

'Come here, my child!' Sally went quickly to the bedside. She put her hand over the thin hand lying on the coverlet.

'I'm so glad you're going to be all right, Aunt Agatha,' she whispered. 'Just go to sleep now and I'll come and see you again in the morning.'

The old eyes closed but the hand held on to Sally's.

'Don't go, Sally,' the feeble voice whispered. 'Sit there, child. I—I want you to stay at Monk's Hollow. There's—a reason.'

She fell silent and Sally knew, from her breathing, that she was asleep. She sat on the chair beside the bed, the old hand in her own, not heeding the cramp in her leg.

Martin came to her side. 'You ought to go now, miss,' she said, but Sally only shook her head.

'I'd rather stay,' she said.

'But the doctor said—'

'I'm not disturbing her. I promise I'll go if she wakes and wants to talk.'

Martin had to be content with that. As the woman walked towards the door Sally thought she saw, on her face, a bitter brooding look as if she was angry about something. But it might only have been the play of shadow in the dark room.

14

'I Need You Here, Sally!'

Sally wakened late. She had stayed with her great-aunt until the old lady, refreshed from her sleep, had wakened. Then Martin had come and had insisted on her going back to her own room. Aunt Agatha had backed her companion up.

'You look tired out, child,' she had said weakly. 'I'll see you in the morning.'

Sally had been glad to climb back into bed. She felt exhausted. Almost at once she had sunk into a deep sleep. Now, awake at last, she lay looking up at the ceiling and wondering what she ought to do.

She had meant to leave Monk's Hollow early today. Now because of her aunt's accident, she must at least stay until the doctor pronounced the old lady to be out of danger.

Presently she got out of bed and went along to the bathroom. Lying in the hot water she decided she would remain until the following day. By that time the doctor would surely know whether her aunt was fit to be left or not.

Returning to her room she dressed then went downstairs. She felt hungry and hoped that breakfast would not have been cleared away.

As she was crossing the hall she heard the bell ring. Briggs appeared almost immediately and crossed to the front door.

Sally making for the dining-room looked curiously at the short middle-aged man who entered the house handing his bowler to the old servant.

'I have come on Mrs Pentland's instructions,' Sally heard him say. 'I'm Mr Morris, her solicitor.'

'Yes, sir. I believe she is expecting you,' Briggs answered and helped the newcomer off with his coat.

Sally's heart quickened. Why had Aunt Agatha sent for her solicitor like this? Was it because she had made up her mind who her heir was to be and wanted to make her will without further delay? It looked very much like it.

Alec and Colin were just finishing their breakfast as Sally went into the dining-room. Alec jumped up and pulled out a chair for her at the big table.

'How are you this morning?' he asked, his lean tanned face anxious as he looked at her.

'I'm fine,' she smiled. 'And very hungry!'

He grinned. 'Well, we can soon put that right,' he said. 'There's bacon and sausage. How does that sound?'

'Wonderful!'

As he went to the sideboard the door opened and Briggs accompanied by Mr Morris, the solicitor, came into the room.

151

The old servant looked at Sally.

'This is Mrs Pentland's solicitor, Miss,' he said. 'He's been travelling from London since early this morning. I asked him if he'd like some breakfast.'

'My name is Morris,' the newcomer smiled, coming forward and shaking hands with Sally. He had bright blue eyes which twinkled at her from behind horn-rimmed glasses. 'I imagine you must be my client's great-niece?'

'Yes, I'm Sally Morgan,' Sally admitted. 'And this is Mr Colin Brent and this Mr Alec Carpenter.'

The little man shook hands with the two younger men, favouring each with a keen glance. Alec, who had put Sally's plate before her, offered to get him something.

'The servant told me that your aunt had an accident last night which might have proved fatal,' Mr Morris said.

'Yes, it was nearly a tragedy,' Alec said pouring coffee at the sideboard. 'Fortunately Miss Morgan went to her great-aunt's room at the right moment and carried her into the corridor.'

'A very brave deed, if I may say so,' the solicitor declared.

Sally, turning to look at Colin, saw

that he was regarding the solicitor with an anxious frown. It flashed across her mind that he was probably wondering whose name this man would presently be entering on her aunt's will as her principal beneficiary.

'And how is Mrs Pentland this morning after her ordeal?' Mr Morris asked.

'I gather she's had quite a good night,' Alec replied. 'Perhaps when the doctor comes he will give us an up to date report.'

Sitting there, listening to the desultory conversation between the three men, Sally thought how upset she had been less than twelve hours ago when she had screamed after seeing the cowled figure outside the sitting-room window. How unimportant it seemed now that nobody had believed her. Something much more significant had happened since. The ghost—or whatever it was she had seen—didn't seem to matter any more.

The door opened and Martin, as formidable as ever in her black dress with her hair strained back from her forehead, appeared. Sally, looking up, saw that for a moment her eyes went to Mr Morris and that a little quiver disturbed the thin line of her grim mouth.

'Mrs Pentland wishes to see you, miss,' she said, glancing at Sally. 'Will you come now, please?'

'How is she this morning, Martin?' Colin asked, lighting a cigarette and blowing the smoke towards the ceiling.

'As well as can be expected, sir,' Martin replied, looking at him disapprovingly as he flicked his spent match towards the fireplace and missed by several feet.

'Has the doctor been yet?' Alec put in.

'Not yet, sir. And now, miss, if you've finished your breakfast—'

Sally got up at once. She looked at the solicitor.

'Shall I tell my aunt you are here?' she asked.

Mr Morris nodded. 'Yes, my dear, if you'd be so kind. Tell her she needn't see me until she feels better. I'm in no hurry.'

Sally went from the room and followed her aunt's companion upstairs. The woman did not speak but walked ahead, back erect, chin in the air. But at the door of her mistress's room she looked at Sally.

'Don't stay with her too long, miss,' she

said. 'She's still suffering from shock; and she's very, very tired.'

'I won't! You can trust me,' Sally murmured, then as Martin stood aside, she went forward into the darkened room.

'Is it you, Sally?' a feeble voice called from the bed.

'Yes, Aunt Agatha. You sent for me.'

'Come over here where I can see you, dear.'

Sally went forward and stood by the bed. The bright eyes in the wrinkled old face looked up at her from the pillow.

'How are you feeling this morning?' she asked.

'Not too bad, love.' A thin hand came from under the bedclothes and took Sally's. 'Sit down beside me, Sally. There's something I want to say to you.'

Sally did as she was told. When she was seated the old woman, with a frightened look round the big shadowy room, said in little more than a whisper:

'Are we alone?'

Sally nodded. 'Yes. Martin showed me into the room then went away.'

'I wanted to talk to you alone, Sally. This is for your ears alone, you understand?'

Greatly mystified Sally nodded. 'What is

it, Aunt Agatha? I don't think you ought to excite yourself—'

The thin hand tightened on hers. The whisper was fiercer now:

'Listen, Sally. I must say what I have to say quickly before we are interrupted.'

'But what is it, Aunt Agatha? What can you have to say that is so important?'

'First I want to thank you for saving my life. It was a very brave deed. I'll always be grateful to you. I didn't deserve what you did after the way I treated your father and mother.'

'All that's in the past, Aunt Agatha.' Sally looked longingly at the door as if willing Martin to appear and rescue her from her predicament.

'But I didn't send for you just to thank you,' the old voice went on. 'I want you to know something, something very important. Someone tried to kill me last night, Sally.'

Sally looked aghast into the lined old face. What was the old women saying? Was she suffering from hallucinations? Old people did go queer at times and get persecution complexes. Perhaps this had happened to Aunt Agatha.

'I'm sure you're wrong, Aunt Agatha,'

she said gently. 'Just try and go to sleep. You'll feel much better when you wake.'

'You think I'm going mad, don't you, girl?' The voice was sharper now, more the voice of the Agatha Pentland of Christmas Eve. 'Well, you're wrong, Sally. They said my bed caught fire because I was smoking. But last night I didn't smoke in bed. I couldn't! I hadn't any cigarettes.'

There was silence in the room only broken when a coal burning in the grate collapsed with a small crash.

'I only found out I'd smoked my last cigarette when Martin had left me by myself,' Aunt Agatha went on. 'I wondered whether to ring then, as I felt so terribly sleepy, I decided to go to sleep instead. The next I knew I was in this bed with the doctor bending over me.'

'But—but, Aunt Agatha, you might have been mistaken,' Sally said slowly. 'Perhaps there was just one cigarette and you've forgotten about it.'

'Nonsense! Besides, I don't usually go to sleep so soon. I usually lie awake watching the firelight on the ceiling. That's when I like to smoke. Old people don't need as much sleep as young, Sally, as you'll learn for yourself one day. But last night

157

I didn't lie for more than a moment or so. I fell deeply asleep, which makes me wonder if someone didn't put a sleeping tablet or two in my bedtime drink then set fire to my bed to make it appear that I'd gone to sleep with a lighted cigarette in my hand.'

'But—I can't believe it!' Sally whispered, her head spinning.

'Why not? Someone knocked Helen out, didn't they? Whoever did such a wicked thing is quite capable of setting an old woman's bed on fire, believe me.'

'But why would they do it?'

'I'm a rich woman, Sally, and I'm just about to make my will. That might have something to do with it.'

'But—Helen—'

'She might be my heir. She was probably knocked over the head to drive her away from Monk's Hollow.'

Sally sat there, silent. It couldn't be true. Aunt Agatha must have been smoking and must have forgotten. No one would surely try to murder her. It just wasn't possible.

She felt the thin fingers tighten again round her own.

'Don't go back to London yet, Sally,' the old voice said and now it was full of appeal. 'I need you here. You will stay, won't you?'

There was nothing for it but to agree. A little of the strain left the old woman's face. She closed her eyes.

'You're my only relative, Sally,' came in a whisper from the colourless lips. 'I want you here. This is—your home.'

Sally, after sitting by the sleeping old woman's side for five more minutes, crept to the door. Only as she left the room did she remember that she had completely forgotten to tell her Aunt Agatha about the arrival of the solicitor.

15

A New Will

Sally went along to her room and sat there for a little while. She felt she could not face the others after the things Aunt Agatha had said to her.

Why, she asked herself over and over again, should anyone want to kill the old lady? Aunt Agatha thought it was something to do with her making a new will.

Yet if she hadn't as yet made the will why should one of those who might possibly benefit from any change want her out of the way before the will was drawn up and signed? It didn't make sense.

Mildred, the maid, came into the room to make the bed. She drew back seeing Sally sitting by the window.

'I'm sorry, miss,' she said. 'I thought the room was empty.'

'That's all right, Mildred,' Sally smiled. 'I'm just going downstairs again.'

The little maid, crossing to the fireplace to clean out the ashes and lay another fire, glanced at the dressing-table which still stood across the wall mirror.

'I often wondered why you moved that heavy piece of furniture, miss,' she said. 'Didn't you like it where it was standing before?'

It was on the tip of Sally's tongue to tell this girl, who seemed a sympathetic little soul, all about the secret passage and how, early on Christmas Day, she had had a mysterious visitor. Then she decided against it. She could not be sure that Mildred would not pass the story on to another servant and it would not be long before it was all over the house.

'It gets more light from the window in its new position,' she said and made for the door.

But before she reached it Mildred called after her:

'I meant to ask you something, miss,' she said hesitantly, and as Sally turned 'I—I'm scared, miss.'

'Scared!' Sally frowned. 'But what are you scared of, Mildred?'

'It's this house, miss,' the little maid said, and with a shiver: 'I sleep at the back. Sometimes in the night I hear someone moving about. I mentioned it to Mrs Martin, who's the housekeeper as well as Madam's companion, but she only laughed and told me I was imagining things.'

'Any old house like this must be full of creaks, especially at night, Mildred,' Sally said, hoping her voice sounded reassuring.

So Mildred had heard something. Could it be the mysterious visitor who had come along the secret passage to this room?

'I think I shall give my notice in, miss,' Mildred said a trifle defiantly. 'I can get plenty of jobs nearer town. There's nothing to do at nights at Monk's Hollow, even when I'm allowed time off, which isn't often.'

Sally said a few more words, praising the little maid's work and saying she was sure her great-aunt appreciated her. Then she left the room and went downstairs.

The first person she saw was Colin. He was standing in the hall looking out of one of the windows beside the front door.

'It's snowing as hard as ever,' he said gloomily. 'Doesn't look as if we'll get out much today. As a matter of fact, I was half-hoping I'd be able to go back to London—'

'I'm sure my great-aunt would rather you stayed—at least until tomorrow,' Sally said.

'How is she?'

'She seems more herself this morning. When I left her she was asleep.'

Colin frowned. 'I can never understand how people manage to set their beds on fire when they smoke a cigarette. I suppose the glowing end must get into the mattress and go on smouldering. But you'd think it would go out if it was deprived of air.'

Mr Morris came out of the dining-room at that moment. He caught sight of Sally.

'Did you speak to Mrs Pentland about my arrival?' he asked.

'I'm afraid I didn't,' she replied. 'Before I could tell her she had fallen asleep.'

'Never mind! I'll seek out her companion and see when it will be convenient for me to interview her.'

Sally went into the sitting-room and sat before the fire. Trevor and Alec were there and they both questioned her eagerly as to how she had found the old lady.

'Where's Helen?' Sally asked.

'She's staying in bed,' Trevor said with a frown. 'She says there's nothing to get up for now it's started snowing again.'

He buried himself in the paperback he was reading. Alec winked at Sally as if to warn her that the subject of Helen was a sore one with her fiancé.

Presently they heard voices in the hall and knew that the doctor had come. Later, Mr Morris came into the room.

'I have spoken to the doctor,' he said. 'Mrs Pentland, I am glad to say, is well on the way to recovery. I have had a little chat with her and she has asked me to say that she hopes that you will all stay on, at least until tomorrow.'

Trevor closed his book abruptly. 'It's not very convenient for me,' he frowned. 'I have a job to go to in the morning. My people won't take too kindly to my losing a day's work—'

'Mrs Pentland asked me to say,' Mr Morris went on, 'that if anyone suffered expense by staying at Monk's Hollow another day, she would gladly defray it. I am sure, Mr Carley, that any salary loss you suffer would gladly be made up by my client.'

'Well, that's different,' Trevor said rather ungraciously. 'I suppose it's all right to stay in that case.'

Colin came into the room at that moment. He looked across at the solicitor.

'Has Mrs Pentland made her will yet?' he asked abruptly. 'I imagine that you've come to Monk's Hollow for that purpose.'

A little of Mr Morris's benevolence faded for a moment as he looked at the young man through his horn-rimmed glasses.

'Mrs Pentland has had precious little time to make a will after last night's unfortunate happenings,' he said. 'I have just seen her. She hopes to talk to me again this evening. Whether it will be about the will, I am not sure.'

'When we arrived on Christmas Eve we were told that we'd been invited to Monk's Hollow because the old lady wanted to see us before she picked her heir and made a will,' Colin persisted. 'It isn't unreasonable that I should be interested in knowing if she's made her mind up, is it? I'm only putting into words what all the others are thinking.'

Mr Morris's smile returned. The gleam of a gold tooth showed as his lips parted.

'I see your point, Mr Brent,' he said pleasantly. 'I'll let you into a secret. Mrs Pentland will be instructing me about drawing up a new will tonight. I shall return to London with those instructions tomorrow morning and I hope she will be able to sign the new will later this week.'

'So until the new will is signed the old one will apply?' Trevor put in.

Mr Morris frowned. 'I don't think I can discuss my client's affairs any more at this stage. If you'll excuse me I'll go to my room.'

When he had gone Colin whistled and looked at the others with a grin.

'Don't look at me so disapprovingly,' he

said. 'I was only finding out what you all wanted to know.'

Trevor, brows knitted, muttered: 'I wonder who would have benefited if the old girl had died in the fire last night. It makes you think, doesn't it?'

Sally bit her lip. So perhaps her great-aunt's fear that someone had tried to murder her was not as outrageous as she had thought.

For obviously if a new will was made leaving the money to Helen, Colin, Alec or herself the other person who might have come into the fortune if she and the others had never come to Monk's Hollow for Christmas would find themselves left out in the cold.

Suddenly she turned and made for the door. She must be alone to think this out. Remembering that Mildred was probably still in her room she made for the little cloakroom near the front door where she had left her heavy coat and shoes.

A few moments later, a scarf over her hair, she opened the front door.

Snow blew in her face as she left the house. But she did not heed it as, her feet sinking into the white carpet, she set off down the drive towards the road.

16

Lost

At first the cold air was exhilarating. Sally, tramping through the crisp fresh snow, enjoyed the exercise. It was nice to get out after being cooped up in the house for so long. It was nice, too, to get away from the others for a bit. She wanted to be alone so that she could think out everything that had happened and get her impressions into some sort of order.

That something strange was happening at Monk's Hollow there could be no doubt. But what was it? Had her great-aunt been right in believing that someone had tried to harm her? Had Trevor hit the nail on the head when he had questioned who would have benefited if Aunt Agatha had died on the previous night?

A shiver that was not entirely due to the bitter cold of the day ran through Sally. She wished suddenly that she could walk right away from Monk's Hollow and never return. Yet that was impossible. Aunt Agatha was her only living relative. The old lady had appealed to her to stay on at the house and she had given her word. No! As soon as she had had her walk and put her mind in some sort of order she would return and stay as long as Aunt Agatha wanted her.

At some point she must have left the winding drive for the trees seemed closer together at this point viewed through the whirling snow. She turned to retrace her steps but it was difficult to see her faint tracks with the snow driving into her face and blinding her.

She stood there for a moment feeling rather scared, then she laughed. She had come out for a walk and she meant to have one. It was nonsense to think, when she was only a few hundred yards from the house, that she was lost.

It would perhaps be as well, though, if she did find the drive and go down to the road. There would then be no question of her making a safe return to the house in due course.

It was dark under the trees. The snow lay thicker than any foliage and the lowering sky above, heavy with more snow to come, permitted only a kind of twilight even though it was not yet midday.

Sally plodded on. Surely, at any moment, she should come out of the trees on to the drive again. But if anything the wood seemed to grow thicker and the snow underfoot deeper. A low branch which she did not see tore the scarf from her head as she blundered on.

With a little cry she turned and groped for it in the snow. She began to feel really frightened now. It was obvious that she had missed her way and that she was heading in a different direction from when she had started out earlier.

She stood still and considered what she should do. She must not panic. Yet, as she stood there in the semi-darkness under the trees, with the snow driving into her face, it was hard not to feel frightened. She had completely lost her sense of direction. Whichever way she took was likely to be the wrong one and the grounds round Monk's Hollow were extensive. In this whirling snowstorm she might walk for hours in circles and never find the house.

She began bitterly to regret coming out at all. For the first time she realised how terribly cold the air was. True, she was wearing a thick coat but it did little to keep out the intense cold, and her feet, because the snow had got into her shoes, felt like ice.

But she went on. She knew that it was useless to stay where she was. Though she might not find the house she might run up against a fence or a wall and be able to follow it round until she came to the road.

But the trees seemed to stretch ahead of her interminably. She began to grow dizzy as the icy wind whirled the snow around her. She was tired too. Once, when she stumbled and fell on her hands and knees, she longed to lower herself full length in the snow and rest for a while. But she knew that that might prove fatal.

She struggled up and made through the trees once more. But every few seconds she had to stop and get her breath. During one of these rests, as she leaned against a tree, she looked back the way she had come.

Just for a moment she thought she saw a movement in the trees a few yards away. She put her almost frozen hands to her face and rubbed her eyes, but when she looked again there was nothing there, only the snow being driven through the trees by the cutting wind.

She staggered on. Was she beginning to see things now? She had often read that travellers, lost in the icy wastes of the Arctic, imagined they saw things that were not there.

Once or twice she glanced back over her shoulder. Once she was quite sure that she saw something move in the trees about twenty yards behind. A little sob rose in her throat. Was she imagining that someone was following her—or was it real?

She broke into a run, an agonised sob rising in her throat. Her legs felt like lead. She could hardly lift them out of the snow. Sooner or later she would come to a full stop, then whoever or whatever it was behind would catch up with her!

Suddenly she found herself at the edge of the trees. Ahead was a whirling wilderness of snowflakes under the leaden sky. Sally hesitated. Should she plunge across the trackless field or dodge back into the shelter of the trees?

She glanced back over her shoulder. She knew that whichever way she went she was almost exhausted and could not keep on her feet more than a few more minutes. She must find somewhere to shelter from the icy wind. All feeling seemed to have left her feet and hands. It could only be a matter of minutes before she dropped helpless on to the snow.

She stood there, holding her breath. Had she imagined that someone was following her? So far no one had come out of the trees in pursuit. Either her eyes had played tricks or whoever had been following her had lost her trail in the storm.

Then her heart gave a great lurch. For a tall figure had come out of the trees a few yards away and was looking straight at her.

With a little cry she turned and started to run back into the trees. But she did not see a trailing root that lay in her path. Tripping her, it sent her sprawling in the snow. She lay, her breath coming in great gulps, panic sweeping through her as the man's tall figure caught her and stood over her.

'Sally!'

As she recognised his voice she looked up into his face, unable to believe that it was really Alec standing by her side. In the poor light she could only see his powerful figure towering above her like a giant. His hair and eyebrows thick with snow were white as an old man's. Even the contours of his face seemed to have been altered by the driving snow.

He bent down and took her frozen hands in his, raising her gently to her feet.

'I called after you, Sally,' he said, 'but you didn't seem to hear. It was a nightmare. I kept losing you in the trees. I had almost given up hope of catching up with you when you stopped on the edge of the trees.'

He held her close and she was content just to stand there with his arms about her. A wave of thankfulness swept over her. Now everything would be all right! Alec would know the way back. Soon they would be in the house once more able to get warm and into dry clothes once again.

But Alec's next words sent a stab of dismay through her.

'I'm as lost as you are, I'm afraid, Sally,' he said. 'When you went out of the sitting-room I followed a minute or so later. I realised you must have left the house and knowing how it was snowing I decided to go after you. I had a feeling you might get lost. I just grabbed a coat and ran for it. I found where your footprints left the drive and followed under the trees. At one point I lost you altogether but I kept on and picked up your tracks again after a few minutes. I suppose I was so intent on following you that I didn't pay too much heed to the direction I'd come from.'

'What had we better do?' Sally asked, looking up into his face.

'We'd better find somewhere to rest, somewhere out of the storm,' he said. 'You look about all in. Once you've had a rest and got a little warmer we'll set off and try to find the house again.'

Sally looked hopelessly at the driving snow and shivered.

'But where can we possibly shelter?' she asked, trying to hide from him that her teeth were chattering almost uncontrollably.

He shielded his eyes with his hand and peered out into the white wilderness away from the trees. 'I may be imagining things, but there seems to be a sort of bulky object somewhere out there,' he said. 'What do you think, Sally?'

She narrowed her eyes against the driving

174

snow and peered out in the direction he had indicated. At first she could see nothing, then, just for a second, she seemed to see something dark like a shadow behind the whirling white flakes.

'I'm not sure—' she began uncertainly but, his hand under her elbow, he drew her away from the trees and started with her across the open space which lay before them.

Sally felt she could hardly put one foot before the other. But she knew she must go on. Over and over again she told herself that everything was going to be all right now that Alec had come. She wasn't alone any more.

Suddenly a small square building loomed up before them.

'It looks like a shepherd's hut,' Alec said, a hint of excitement in his voice. 'It won't have any home comforts I'm afraid, but if we could get into it we could at any rate get out of the reach of this frightful wind.'

Still holding her by the arm he drew her on in a circuit of the little stone hut. Presently they saw a wooden door. Alec tried to open it. His face fell when he found it to be locked.

'We must get in,' he muttered and, raising his foot, he delivered a heavy kick which, to Sally's relief, sent the door flying open. There was a warm smell of hay inside, though it was too dark at first to see any details of the hut's interior. There came the scrape of a match and by the light of the flickering flame Sally saw that the hut was empty except for a pile of hay in one corner, and what appeared to be some wooden sheep hurdles reared against one wall.

'Can you bear it if I leave the door open for a few more minutes?' Alec asked, glancing at Sally. 'I've had an idea.'

It was almost too cold to speak. She muttered something and nodded. Crossing to one of the wooden hurdles he placed it on the ground and examined it. He nodded as if satisfied.

'I think this will do,' he muttered, and brought his foot down sharply on the crossbar.

At first it did not give but after he had stamped on it several times it cracked and then gave way. Collecting a little pile of hay from the corner he brought it over to the opposite wall. Striking a match he set the hay on fire and, as it flared up, fed the smallest pieces of wood to the flames. When the fire was going nicely he closed the door and turned to Sally again. 'If we can keep this fire going we shall probably get warm,' he said.

He fetched another of the hurdles over so that she could sit on it and hold out her hands to the fire. Gradually the warmth began to thaw her frozen limbs and her teeth stopped chattering. Alec, going on one knee, raised her foot and unlaced her shoe.

'You'd be better without these,' he said and began to massage her stockinged feet vigorously.

'Feeling warmer now?' he asked, looking up at her, the firelight glowing on his face.

She nodded. 'I don't know what I would have done if you hadn't come along when you did, Alec,' she said quietly.

He fed more wood to the flames before he spoke again. Then he asked quietly: 'Why did you go out at all, Sally? It was rather a mad thing to do in the storm, wasn't it?'

'I suppose it was,' she replied, 'but I felt I couldn't stay in the house another moment. I felt I could hardly breathe.'

'I think I know what you mean. Things have been getting on top of all of us during the last day or so.' Then he added cheerfully: 'But we only have to be patient for a little time longer now. Tonight your aunt will make her new will and then we'll be able to go our various ways again.'

She did not say anything to that, but to her dismay she felt two tears roll slowly down her cheeks. She wondered why she felt as she did. Was it exhaustion—or was it because she realised that when she left Monk's Hollow she was unlikely to see Alec Carpenter again?

To her relief he did not seem to have seen the tears. As he stared down into the flames, rubbing his hands vigorously to restore the circulation, he was smiling.

'You know, Sally, New Zealand seems a part of another world just now,' he said.

'You must wish you were back there, and that you'd never left it,' she murmured.

Suddenly he looked into her face. His eyes were very serious when next he spoke.

'I don't think that at all, Sally,' he said in a low voice. 'You see, if I hadn't left New Zealand and come to England I—I'd never have met you.'

17

Aunt Agatha's Decision

Sally felt the colour creep into her cheeks at Alec's words. What did he mean? Surely—surely he couldn't have fallen in love with her. Why, they hardly knew each other.

She looked into the heart of the fire again. After a few moments she felt Alec's hand close over hers.

'Sally, you'd like it in New Zealand,' he said in his deep attractive voice. 'The people are very English in their outlook and the countryside is very beautiful.'

'But—but what leads you to believe I might want to go to New Zealand?' she asked, and felt angry with herself because her voice was trembling so.

'I thought you might consider going back with me, as my wife,' he said, and slowly she looked away from the fire and into his eyes again.

So he was proposing to her! It was so

179

unexpected, coming on top of all that she had gone through in the last hour, that she just stared at him in bewilderment as if she could not take in the implication of what he had said. His hand tightened on hers.

'I'm sorry, Sally,' he said contritely. 'I shouldn't have sprung it on you like that, but I do love you. I—I can't bear to think of you going back to London without knowing how I feel.'

'But I—never expected—' she whispered, exhaustion sweeping over her once again so that she felt limp and weak.

He put more wood on the fire. Very quietly he said:

'Don't think any more about it now, Sally. I know it wasn't fair of me to take you off your guard like this when you're feeling wet, cold and miserable. If you choose to forget what I've said I shall understand. In any case, I never hoped that you would feel the same way that I did. It was only a dream, a beautiful dream I had.'

She wanted to put out her hand and take his again, tell him that if he would only be patient, give her time, she would think over what he had said. But suddenly he got to his feet and went to the door. Opening it an inch or two he looked out.

'It's grown a lot lighter,' he said, 'and I do believe the snow is not quite as thick as before. Once it stops we can try to find our way back to the house.'

He joined her by the fire again. It was as if he had not ever spoken about anything but the snow and their predicament. They sat in silence for a while. Sally felt her head nodding. She fought off the waves of sleep that threatened to wash over her but it was difficult keeping her eyes open.

Suddenly she felt Alec's hand on her arm, urging her to her feet. He led her in a daze across the hut to the sweet smelling hay in the far corner.

'Just you lie down there for a few minutes and close your eyes, Sally,' he said gently. 'You might as well have a little sleep. It will do you more good than crouching over this fire.'

She was too tired to resist and sank with a sigh on to the soft hay. She saw Alec taking off his coat and a moment later he had wrapped it around her. She made a feeble protest but he did not heed her.

'I'll sit by the fire while you have your rest,' he said, and, as she closed her eyes, he moved away to the other side of the hut.

She intended only to relax for a few minutes but after a few seconds, or so it seemed, she felt someone shaking her shoulder.

She looked up in surprise into Alec's smiling face. The door behind him was wide open and she could see a fitful gleam of sun on the shining snow beyond.

'Wake up!' he cried. 'You've been asleep nearly two hours. The snow's stopped and we've a good chance of finding our way back to the house now.'

She sat up and rubbed her eyes. It seemed impossible that she had been asleep more than a second or two. But as she got to her feet she realised how rested she was. She saw that the fire had gone out, probably because there was no more wood to burn.

She gave Alec his coat back and he shrugged into it.

'Are you quite warm?' he asked and she nodded.

'Then we'd better go,' he said, and made for the door. As she followed she wondered if she had dreamed that he had proposed to her earlier. Just now he was so matter of fact about everything that it seemed impossible he had told her he loved her and wanted her to marry him and go back to New Zealand.

Outside Alec stood looking at the sun low on the horizon, whose slanting rays fell across the snow. He nodded with satisfaction.

'I've a fairly good idea where we are now,' he said. 'The sun's almost in the south, which means that the house is behind us. We'll have to go through the trees again but this time I don't think we'll get lost.'

'What time is it?' Sally asked.

He glanced at his watch. 'About half past three,' then added with a grin: 'We should just be back in time for a cup of tea. I think we could both do with one.'

They said little as they tramped through the snow. Sally, as they went through the trees, thought once again of the terror she had experienced when she had known she was lost in the blinding snowstorm whirling all about her. She glanced at Alec. But for this man she might have been lying under a snowdrift, freezing to death at this very moment. Even if a search party had come out from the house they would have had little chance of finding her in such conditions.

As if conscious of her glance Alec looked sideways at her. He gave her a warm smile.

'It won't be long now,' he said encouragingly and slipped his arm through hers to help her along.

Five minutes later they came out of the trees to find Monk's Hollow straight ahead of them. A little despondent group was standing in front of the house. It consisted of Colin, Trevor and Mr Morris, the solicitor. They were all wearing hats and coats and had obviously been searching the grounds.

Colin was the first to see Alec and Sally emerge from the trees. He gave a sudden shout.

'There they are!' he cried and making towards them, 'Where have you two been? We've looked everywhere for you. We were just about to call out the local constabulary.'

'I'll explain later,' Alec said, pushing past. 'Sally's exhausted. She needs a hot drink and food.'

A little bewildered the three men followed them into the house. A big fire was burning in the sitting-room and Alec, helping Sally out of her coat, sat her in front of it and rang the bell. Presently Mildred appeared. He told her to bring hot coffee and cut some sandwiches and the girl, after a scared glance at Sally, hurried away.

'And now, Mr Carpenter, perhaps you'll tell us what happened,' Mr Morris said, coming forward.

Quickly Alec explained how he had missed Sally and had followed her into the snow.

'By sheer good fortune we stumbled on a shepherd's hut and sheltered there until the snow stopped,' he said. 'As soon as I was able to get a bearing by the sun we were able to return to the house.'

'How's Aunt Agatha?' Sally asked, looking up at Colin.

'I think she's been sleeping most of the day,' he replied. 'The doctor came again about an hour and a half ago and seemed quite satisfied.'

A few minutes later Mildred came into the room carrying a well-loaded tray. Sally, seeing the food, realised for the first time how terribly hungry she was. She and Alec started in on the sandwiches and neither

185

had much to say to the others until all the food had disappeared. Half-way through her second cup of hot sweet coffee Sally looked at Alec.

'I haven't thanked you properly yet for saving my life, Alec,' she said.

He looked a little embarrassed at her words. 'Oh, it was nothing. I suppose if you'd gone on a few more yards you'd have found that hut for yourself, and sheltered until you were able to get back to the house.

But she shook her head. 'I'm sure I shouldn't, Alec, and you must know that too. I was at the end of my tether. If you hadn't come when you did I think I should just have wandered off into the snow until I fell exhausted.'

Trevor nodded approvingly. 'You're certainly a resourceful sort of chap, Alec, though you must admit you were lucky to find those sheep hurdles to hand when you wanted to make a fire.'

'I'd be the first to admit that,' Alec laughed, then turned as the door opened and Martin, Mrs Pentland's companion appeared.

'My mistress wishes to speak to you, sir,' she said looking at the solicitor.

Mr Morris got to his feet. 'I will come along immediately,' he said and followed the woman from the room.

'The old girl must have wakened up,' Colin said lighting a cigarette. 'Perhaps she's decided to make her new will immediately.'

'Well, if she has, you'll be out of your misery one way or the other very shortly, won't you?' Trevor said and Sally heard the faint sneer in his voice.

She began to wonder where Helen was. Perhaps she was staying in her own room so that she would not have to bicker with Trevor any more.

Presently the solicitor returned. His face was solemn.

'My client has asked me to invite you all to go to her room,' he said. 'Perhaps you, Mr Carley, will ask your fiancée to join us there.'

Colin nervously threw his cigarette into the fire.

'I wonder what she wants to see us for,' he muttered, then, looking at Trevor: 'Aren't you going to fetch Helen, then? The old lady's waiting for us.'

Trevor, biting his lip, turned away without a word, but it was obvious that he did not like being ordered about by Colin.

'Shall we go upstairs?' Mr Morris said, and made for the door.

The others followed him out into the hall. Sally still felt weak and shaky and Alec, perhaps guessing this, took her arm and smiled down at her.

'You feeling all right, Sally?' he asked.

She smiled back at him. 'Yes, I'm fine. But I shan't be sorry to go to bed tonight, I must admit.'

Following the solicitor they went upstairs and along the passage towards Mrs Pentland's room. Here Mr Morris knocked on the door which was almost immediately opened by Martin.

'Come in!' the woman said, and stood aside as they walked past her and grouped themselves around the bed.

Sally drew a sharp breath of pity as she looked at the old woman propped up against the pillows. In the last few hours the old lady seemed to have aged considerably. Her face seemed more lined than ever, her eyes more deeply sunken in their sockets.

There was silence for a moment or two, then the old lady spoke.

'Where are Helen and her fiancé?' she asked sharply.

'They should be coming at any moment, Mrs Pentland,' Mr Morris said soothingly, then turned, relieved, as there was knock at the door and Martin admitted the late-comers.

As they joined the circle round the bed the old lady looked from one face to another. Sally wondered if she knew anything about her and Alec's adventure in the snow but as she did not speak of it she concluded that no one had told her, probably because she was too ill to be worried with such news.

'You will remember when you arrived at Monk's Hollow on Christmas Eve,' the old lady said, 'that I told you I should be making a new will in favour of one of you. That is why I have asked my good friend, Mr Morris, to come to Monk's Hollow at Christmas, although I knew it would be a great inconvenience for him to leave his own family at such a time.'

Mr Morris shook his head with a smile. 'I was very happy to come, Madam, as well you know,' he declared.

The old lady raised her hand. 'That's as maybe. Anyhow, I'm afraid you've had a wasted journey. I've changed my mind about making a new will.'

For a moment there was dead silence in the room, then Helen, who looked pale and tired, Sally thought, said a little sharply:

'Do you mean that—well, you don't like any one of us better than another?'

Mrs Pentland nodded, a trifle defiantly.

'You can put it like that if you like. I'm sorry to have troubled you all but—well, there it is.'

Colin laughed a little harshly. 'Then there really isn't much point in us staying at Monk's Hollow any longer?'

The old lady met his glance with a stony stare.

'I suppose not. I shall send each of you a cheque to your home address to make up in some measure for your disappointment. It will be quite generous, I promise. And, now, I'm feeling tired. I'd be glad to be alone.'

Mr Morris seemed as if he was about to say something, then he turned and made for the door.

First Trevor, then Helen and Colin followed him. As Alec turned away Sally looked back at Aunt Agatha. She was sure there was something wrong. This all seemed to have happened so suddenly, so unexpectedly. But if she hoped that the old lady wanted her to remain for a quiet word she was wrong. Aunt Agatha's eyes were closed as she lay back against the pillows. Sally, after waiting a moment, turned and hurried after Alec.

Martin held the door open to her. Sally, glancing at the woman, saw the thin smile on her lips. Whatever anybody else thought about the old lady's decision it was obvious that her companion was delighted.

18

'Off With the Old Love–'

The short day had come to an end. Darkness had closed down on Monk's Hollow. Inside the house lights had been turned on, curtains drawn across the windows.

Sally, coming out into the corridor outside her great-aunt's room, found Alec waiting for her. The others had disappeared.

'Well, what are you going to do?' he asked, looking at her keenly.

'I don't suppose there's much chance of getting back to London tonight,' she said doubtfully.

He frowned. 'In any case you're not well enough. You've gone through a considerable ordeal today. You ought to go to bed early and have a good night's rest.'

She knew that he was right. Her mind shrank from the thought of a long and tedious journey back to London, even if there were any trains running from Darkling Halt so late on Boxing Day.

'I do feel rather tired,' she admitted, then, looking into Alec's face, she added: 'Why do you think Aunt Agatha's acting like this? I can't think it's simply because she's decided she doesn't like any of us. I couldn't help but feel that—well, she was scared about something.'

He looked at her sharply. 'Scared! Why should she be scared?'

She shrugged. 'I don't know. It's something to do with her will, I'm sure. I stayed behind for a moment when you had gone, hoping she would say something else to me. But she just closed her eyes and turned away. Oh, Alec, I'm worried. After all I'm her only relative. I feel sort of responsible for her, more so than anybody else.'

His eyes softened. He took her hand and pressed it.

'You're tired out, Sally,' he said. 'Everything seems larger than life to you tonight. Go to bed early and have a good night's rest. Everything will seem brighter in the morning.'

She smiled gratefully at him. 'You're very nice to me, Alec. I don't know what I'd have done without you in the last few days.'

He turned away, a shadow crossing his face.

'You mean a great deal to me,' he said quietly, then, as if not trusting himself to say any more, he walked down the corridor and she saw him disappear round the corner beyond which lay the stairs.

She went along to her room. She would take Alec's advice and lie down for a while. She did not feel like meeting the others in any case. She could just imagine how angry Colin and Helen especially would be at the turn events had taken.

When she reached her room a fire was

burning brightly and the curtains had been pulled across the window to shut out the bleak snowy scene outside. The bed beckoned a warm comfortable invitation and Sally did not resist it. In a moment she was under the eiderdown, her fair head on the pillow. Almost instantly she was fast asleep.

In a room not very far away Helen looked angrily at her fiancé.

'I'm not going back to London tonight, Trevor,' she snapped. 'For one thing the roads will be dangerous and for another—'

'For another you're expecting a miracle to happen, aren't you?' he said, contempt in his voice. 'Why can't you realise that the party's over, Helen? The old girl's decided she doesn't like any of you and she's going to leave her money to the proverbial cats' home. Quite honestly, I don't blame her!'

Helen's green eyes blazed. 'That's a nice thing to say to the girl you're supposed to be going to marry, I must say! You don't think I'm good enough to be old Agatha Pentland's heir, then?'

His eyes were uneasy now. 'Well, I didn't quite mean it like that. But I've never understood right from the start why Mrs Pentland should want to leave her money away from the family. She's got a perfectly good niece. Why doesn't she leave her fortune to her?'

'You know very well that she fell out with Sally's father years ago,' Helen snapped. 'She probably thinks Sally's a chip off the old block now she's seen her. I don't think if Sally was my niece—God forbid!—that I'd want to leave her a penny. She's too superior for my liking.'

'You're sure you're not jealous of her?' Trevor asked, a hint of a sneer in his voice. 'I've watched you when you've seen her talking to that Colin Brent! You don't like it when he pays any attention to anybody but yourself, do you?'

Her hand flew out and landed on his cheek with a stinging slap. He fell back with an angry exclamation, his hand to his face.

'What did you do that for?' he demanded angrily.

'Because you'd no right to say such a thing!' she cried. 'Colin Brent means nothing to me. Why should he?'

'But you're not going to deny that you were engaged to him once, are you?'

She eyed him in astonishment. 'Who told you that? I—I—'

'It's no good denying it, Helen. I've known for a long time. We were at a dance once. A man came up to me when you had gone to the cloakroom to ask if you were Helen Renton. When I said you were he asked where your fiancé, Colin Brent, was. I was a bit sharp with him and he went away. I never told you about the incident because I didn't think it was worth bothering about.'

She turned away and looked into the fire. When she did not speak he said urgently:

'Let's go away tonight, Helen. The main roads will be reasonably clear. We can be back in London by ten o'clock. Old Morris, the solicitor, left an hour ago. He didn't seem to mind the weather.'

But she shook her head. 'I'm staying here,' she said stubbornly. 'And now go away. I'm tired. I want to rest.'

He stared at her unresponsive back for several seconds, then, when she still did not turn, he made for the door. But before he could reach it there was a knock. Helen swung round, a frown on her pretty face. Trevor, with a glance at her, turned the handle and opened the door.

Colin Brent was standing there. He looked a little taken aback to find Trevor in Helen's room.

'Yes. What do you want?' Trevor demanded roughly.

'I—I just wanted a word with Helen—' Colin said, for once at a loss.

'She's not available,' Trevor said, glaring at his rival.

Before Colin could speak Helen hurried forward. Completely ignoring her fiancé she smiled at Colin.

'Come in, Colin,' she invited. 'Trevor is just going.'

Trevor, who had kept his temper admirably up to that point, completely lost it now. Seizing Colin's shoulder as he came forward he pushed him violently back so that he found himself in the corridor outside once more.

'Stay away from my fiancée!' he shouted, almost beside himself. 'If you try to get into her room again I'll—'

Colin, who had recovered his balance, came quickly forward. He thrust his face into Trevor's.

'What will you do, little man?' he demanded.

But before Trevor could say anything Helen had shouldered her way between them. 'He'll do nothing at all,' she said, and with a contemptuous glance at her fiancé. 'Go away! I don't want to see you again today.'

He looked from one to the other, fists clenched, eyes blazing, then, as if realising there was nothing he could do now that they were both against him, he turned on his heel, hurried from the room and disappeared towards the stairs.

Colin closed the door after him. 'I'm sorry if I've come at an inconvenient moment,' he said with a grin.

Frowning, she turned back towards the fire. 'It's time Trevor learned that being engaged to him doesn't give him the right to have me always at his beck and call. You'll be interested to know that he's found out that you and I were once going to be married.'

'No wonder he's ratty!' he said. 'You could perhaps have got back into his good books by telling him how glad you were to be able to give me the go-by and accept him. After all, he has a great deal more money than I have, Helen.'

'You needn't be sarcastic with me,

Colin!' she cried. 'I accepted Trevor because I thought I liked him better than you. That was the only reason.'

'And now you've found out that perhaps I wasn't so bad after all, eh?'

When she did not speak he went on in a more serious tone: 'Helen, you don't want to be engaged any longer to that stuffy young man. You're a bit of a vagabond, like me. You were never happier than when you were on the stage, now were you? Confess!'

She bit her lip and said, rather reluctantly: 'I did enjoy the life, I must admit, but I ran out of parts. I just couldn't carry on any longer. And Trevor seemed to offer me a secure life, without having to wonder where the next pound note was coming from.'

He went closer to her. All the banter had gone from his voice now.

'Listen, Helen, there's never been anybody but you for me. I see all your faults but—well, you're still the girl I want.'

She shook her head, tears in her eyes. 'It just wouldn't work out, Colin! You drift from one ill-paid job to another. How on earth could you support me?'

For one moment his eyes glinted angrily.

'I'm not doing as badly as all that. As a matter of fact I've been asked to take part in a television series in the New Year. It might lead to great things. There might even be a small part for you if you play your cards properly.'

She swung round on him, lips parted, eyes sparkling behind her tears.

'Do you really mean it, Colin? Oh, if only I could get back into acting.'

He nodded, and took both her hands in his. 'Charlie Grandage, who's producing the series, would give you the part if I asked him, I know. Is it a deal?'

She nodded. She was almost beside herself with delight now.

'I can hardly wait to get back to London, Colin,' she cried. 'Can't we go tonight?'

He shook his head. 'There's no point in going back immediately. I can't do anything until the New Year in any case. Besides—'

'Besides—what?'

'While there's life there's hope,' he said in a low voice. 'I'm not altogether sure that I believe what the old lady said about not changing her will. I can't really think that she's got us all down here for Christmas just to tell us she's not going to make one of us her heir. I think something else has made her change her mind. I'd like to find out what it is.'

'Do you think you will?' she asked with interest.

He shrugged. 'I don't know. It's worth trying. In any case we can leave tomorrow as easily as tonight. There's always the chance that the old lady may change her mind in the small hours.'

They were standing very close together. Suddenly he took her into his arms and kissed her. She kissed him back with passion.

'Oh, Colin, why did I ever let you go?' she murmured.

He kissed her again. 'Better not try it again. You've got me for life now.'

A few minutes later he left the room. He did not know that Trevor, hiding in the shadows, watched him walk away, a look on his face that would have made Colin feel very uneasy if he had seen it.

19

Accident

Sally wakened feeling hungry. The fire had burned down to red ash and the room felt chilly.

She switched on the light and looked at her watch. Half-past eight! That meant she had been asleep over four hours.

She decided to go downstairs. Dinner would be over by this time but perhaps Briggs would bring her something if she asked him. A sandwich and a glass of milk would do.

She encountered the old servant in the hall and he told her that, although the others had eaten their meal, he had not yet cleared away in the dining-room.

'There's cold turkey, if that suits you, miss,' he said, 'and I can easily get cook to heat up some soup. I'll call you when it's ready.'

Sally, thanking him, turned towards the sitting-room. She found Alec, Colin and

Helen sitting before the fire. Alec who had been reading, jumped up when he saw her with a smile.

'Have you had a good rest?' he asked, and she nodded.

'Briggs is getting me something to eat,' she said. 'I believe you've had your meal?'

'All but Trevor,' Alec replied, and Sally saw Colin and Helen exchange a glance.

'Have you decided what to do about leaving Monk's Hollow?' she asked.

'There's a train at ten o'clock from Darkling Halt,' Alec replied. 'I suppose you and Trevor, Helen, and you, Colin, will be travelling to London by car?'

Colin smiled. 'Yes, I for one hope to be away in good time in the morning.'

At that moment Briggs came to the door and told Sally her supper was ready for her. When she went into the dining-room she was surprised to find Trevor sitting at the long table. Briggs put a plate of soup before each of them.

'I thought you'd have had your meal by this time,' Sally said when the young man did not speak.

Trevor turned a pale strained face to her. His eyes were very unhappy. 'I had other things to do,' he muttered, and went on with his meal.

She wondered what had happened to upset him. Had he quarrelled with Helen? It seemed very much like it. He was obviously trying to avoid her if he waited until she had had her meal before having his own. Deciding it was no business of hers she left him in peace and they finished the meal in silence.

Later, Sally went back to the sitting-room though Trevor disappeared once more. Alec suggested a game of cards to pass the time, but Helen, with an exaggerated yawn, said she was tired and was going to bed. Colin was not long in following her and Alec, when the door closed behind him, gave a little laugh.

'You seem fated to be thrown into my company today, Sally,' he said.

She felt the colour come into her cheeks. The last time they had been alone he had told her he loved her. She wondered if he would consider this the right moment to propose to her again.

She did not know whether to feel relieved or disappointed when he said he thought it was a good time to go up to his room and pack ready to leave in the morning.

'I've asked Briggs to get us a car to

take us to the Halt in good time for the train,' he said. 'I suppose you won't mind travelling with me, Sally?'

'Why should I?' she asked a little sharply. 'It's very good of you to take so much trouble.'

He looked at her a little uncertainly, as if he wanted to say something else, then, turning rather abruptly away, he made for the door.

'Good night!' he said, and she felt the tears prick into her eyes as he disappeared.

She wondered what would have happened if he had grabbed her in his arms and kissed her fiercely and told her that he loved her and would not take no for an answer. Would she have thrown her arms round his neck, glad to surrender to such storm tactics? Or would she have slapped his face and told him she wanted nothing more to do with him?

If only she knew—if only she knew—

She went slowly upstairs. At the top she hesitated. Perhaps she should try to see her great-aunt and have another talk to her. Perhaps the old lady would be alone now and would be more inclined to confide in her than she had felt like doing that afternoon.

But as she approached the bedroom door it opened and Martin came out into the corridor. She looked questioningly at Sally.

'I'd like to see my Aunt Agatha,' Sally said, determined not to be browbeaten by this woman.

But Martin was unexpectedly pleasant and sympathetic. She looked at Sally, genuine regret in her eyes.

'I'm very sorry, Miss Morgan,' she said, 'but your great-aunt has just fallen asleep. She had quite a nasty turn about two hours ago but she seems over it now, though of course she's quite exhausted.'

Looking into the woman's blandly smiling face Sally realised that, short of pushing Martin aside and forcing her way into the room there was nothing she could do.

'Perhaps I could see her for a few minutes before I leave in the morning,' she said, and the woman, still smiling, bid her good night and watched her as she walked away down the corridor.

Perhaps because she was so tired Sally slept dreamlessly that night. Mildred the maid, wakened her with a cup of tea.

'It's quite a nice morning, miss,' she

206

said, drawing the curtains back. Rather wistfully, she added: 'I wish I was going to London with you, miss.'

Sally smiled. 'I must give you my address, Mildred,' she said. 'If you ever do come to London you could look me up.'

'That's real kind of you, miss!' Mildred cried and hurried, bright-eyed and smiling from the room.

When she was dressed Sally went downstairs. She found the three young men having breakfast together. There was no sign of Helen.

'Where's Helen?' she asked, and saw the sudden venomous glance which Trevor threw in Colin's direction.

'Apparently she doesn't want any breakfast,' Colin said. 'She's finishing her packing.'

Sally, who had thought it odd that Colin and not Trevor should answer her question, realised that something was very wrong between the two men. Had Trevor found out that at one time Colin was engaged to Helen? And had they had a terrible row, even broken off their engagement to each other?

But she forgot their troubles in remembering that she was still hoping to see her Aunt Agatha before she left Monk's Hollow for the last time. When she had finished her breakfast she stood up.

'Don't forget that the taxi is coming for us in half an hour,' Alec said.

'I'll be ready,' she said and went from the room.

She went upstairs and along the corridor to her aunt's bedroom. She listened at the door but could hear no sound inside the room. A little nervously she turned the handle and opened the door.

The old lady was lying with closed eyes against her pillows. There was no sign of her companion. With a sigh of relief Sally tiptoed forward and stood by the bed.

'Aunt Agatha!' she said in a low voice and slowly the old eyes opened.

'Sally!' There was fear in the eyes now. 'What are you doing here? I thought you'd gone away.'

'I'm going in a few minutes,' Sally replied. 'I came to say good-bye.'

With a nervous glance towards the door the old woman held out her hand.

'Sally—' she began, and as Sally leaned eagerly forward she opened her mouth as if to say more.

'Yes, what is it, Aunt Agatha?' Sally

asked, when no sound came from the thin puckered lips.

'It's—it's nothing, Sally,' the old lady said. She pressed her great-niece's hand. 'It—it was nice to see you, my dear. You're very much like your father. Good-bye and God bless you.'

Sally, seeing the tears rolling down the faded old cheeks, went on her knees beside the bed.

'Aunt Agatha, what is it?' she asked urgently. 'Something's upsetting you. Why don't you tell me what it is?'

But the old lady, as if making a great effort, drew her hand sharply out of Sally's and turned away.

'Go now, Sally!' she said. 'I'm tired. I want to go to sleep.'

Sally waited a few more seconds, then, as the door opened and Martin came into the room, she got to her feet.

'You know where to find me now, Aunt Agatha,' she said. 'I'll come to you if you send for me at any time,'

But still the old lady did not speak and, with a sigh, Sally turned and made for the door.

Martin held it open for her and closed it behind her with a click as she left the room.

Sad at heart Sally went back to her own room and finished packing her suitcase. Carrying it down to the hall she found Colin and Helen about to leave the house. Colin's car was drawn up at the foot of the steps and as Sally came down the stairs he picked up his own and Helen's suitcase and took it outside.

'Isn't it a glorious day?' Helen asked, looking out at the strong sunlight which shone dazzlingly on the snow.

Sally realised that the other girl was very nervous. Suddenly she knew why. There was no sign of Trevor but it was obvious that Helen was going to London in Colin's car.

'We're off now,' Colin said, and held out his hand to Sally. 'It's been nice meeting you, Sally. Perhaps we might see you in London some time.'

Sally, a little bewildered, shook hands with them both and watched them walk down the steps to the car. Colin, after helping Helen in, seated himself at the wheel. A moment later, with a roar from the powerful engine, the sports car set off down the drive.

'So Helen's gone with Colin, has she?'

It was Alec's voice and Sally turned to him.

'But where's Trevor?' she asked, but before he could reply there came a shattering crash in the distance.

'What was that?'

But Alec, ignoring Sally's question, had already run past her and out on to the snow-covered drive. She followed him. His long legs carried him far ahead as he ran down the drive and out of sight in the trees.

What could have happened? Had Colin and Helen skidded off the drive and into a tree? It seemed very much like it.

Then as she came round a bend in the drive Sally's eyes opened in dismay at the scene that lay before her.

Colin's car had swerved across the drive and now leaned drunkenly against a tree which had stopped it. Its occupants, because it was an open car, had been flung out and now lay motionless in the snow. Slewed across the drive with a crumpled radiator was Trevor's car. Trevor was climbing shakily out of it from behind the driving wheel.

Sally saw that Alec had gone straight to

Helen's side. She did not seem as badly hurt as her companion for, as he bent over her, she raised herself on one elbow and looked round.

'What happened?' Sally asked, coming up.

Trevor did not reply but stood by the side of his car looking across at Alec who was now bending by Colin's side.

Sally went to see if she could help Alec.

'Is he badly hurt?' she asked a little fearfully.

He looked up at her and his eyes were very serious.

'It's hard to say, Sally,' he said quietly. 'We must get him up to the house at once and send for the doctor. He must have hit the tree as he was flung out of the car.'

20

'You Can't Stay Here, Sally!'

The sound of a car coming up the snow-covered drive brought Alec to his feet.

'This must be the taxi I ordered,' he said, a note of relief in his voice. 'You go ahead to the house, Sally, and ring for the doctor. The taxi driver will help me to carry Colin.'

'But should he be moved?' Sally asked with a doubtful glance at the unconscious form lying in the snow.

'He doesn't seem to have any bones broken and I'm sure he'll suffer more by lying in the snow than getting him into the warmth of the house,' Alec said.

Sally turned away. Before she started back to the house she glanced at Trevor, still standing dazed and bewildered, at the side of his damaged car. A little distance away Helen was getting to her feet, holding on to the tree at her side for support.

Sally broke into a run as she made for

213

the house. She wondered how badly hurt Colin was. Suppose—suppose he died!

Briggs looked as her in astonishment as she went into the hall, her face flushed, gasping for breath.

'Why, miss, whatever's happened?' he began but she shook her head impatiently.

'There's been an accident,' she gasped. 'Mr Brent is badly hurt. They're bringing him up to the house now.'

'I—I thought I heard a crash—'

'Tell someone to get Mr Brent's room ready,' Sally ordered and turned towards the telephone. 'I must ring up the doctor. Do you know his number, Briggs?'

The old man made a manful effort to pull himself together. 'It—it's written up at the side of the telephone, miss. Dr Bradley is the name. You've seen him visiting the house—'

'Yes, yes,' Sally said, and hurried across the hall.

She just caught the doctor starting out on his rounds and he promised to go to Monk's Hollow immediately. She put the receiver down and went out into the hall again. She saw Martin coming down the stairs. Briggs had disappeared.

'What is happening?' Mrs Pentland's

companion demanded. 'There was a crash
—'

Sally quickly told her what had happened. The woman frowned.

'I'm not sure that it's wise to move him from what you say,' she said. 'Perhaps I'd better go and see how badly hurt he is.'

She made for the door and Sally followed. But as they went out on to the snowy drive they saw a small procession coming out of the trees. To Sally's relief Colin was being helped along by Alec and the taxi driver. Apparently he had recovered consciousness after she had gone to the house and was now able to walk.

A few yards behind, walking well apart, were Trevor and Helen.

'But I thought—!' Sally cried, as the little party slowly approached.

'He must only have been stunned,' Alec said. 'I thought he'd been flung into the tree but he must have only caught it a glancing blow as he fell. The snow broke his fall, otherwise he would have been seriously hurt.'

Colin, catching Sally's eye, grinned crookedly at her. His face was pale and a thin trickle of blood came from a cut on his forehead.

'My head's harder than my heart,' he said, rather shakily. 'Don't look so tragic, Sally. I'm not going to die this time.'

'Take him into the sitting-room and I'll have a look at him,' Martin said sharply, and turned back towards the house.

Alec and the taxi driver, Colin's arms about their shoulders, followed her without another word. Sally looked at Helen.

'How did it happen?' she asked.

Helen threw a venomous look at Trevor. 'This madman ran into us. It was deliberate! He tried to kill us both, there's no doubt about that.'

Trevor shook his head helplessly. It was obvious to Sally that he was still shocked and in no condition to defend himself against Helen's attack.

'I—I'd been for some petrol in the village,' he muttered. 'When—when I was coming back up the drive Colin's car came towards me like a torpedo. We—we met on the curve and—'

'You know very well that you arranged it like that!' Helen shouted a little hysterically. 'Colin wasn't going as fast as all that. He jammed on his brakes, went into a skid and flew off the road. It's a wonder we weren't both killed.

You did it because you were jealous, and you know it. You were lying in wait—'

'All right, all right,' Sally said soothingly. 'You're both too upset and shaken to think straight at the moment. Let's go into the house. You'll both feel better after a cup of hot coffee.'

Colin had been taken into the sitting-room and was sitting on a seat before the fire. Martin, after a quick examination, told him that he had escaped with nothing worse than a cut on his forehead.

'But you've had a severe shock,' she said. 'I don't think you're fit to drive your car again today.'

Colin gave a short laugh. 'I'm afraid it won't be fit to drive in any case,' he said. 'Thanks to that madman who ran into me I should think it's probably a total write-off.'

Trevor who, with Sally and Helen, had come into the room, seemed about to say something. But at that moment there was the sound of a car coming to a halt outside the door.

'There's the doctor,' Alec said, and went out into the hall as the doctor came into the house.

Helen insisted on staying in the sitting-room while Dr Bradley looked at Colin. Sally persuaded Trevor to go into the dining-room to have some hot coffee. As she poured it for him and added plenty of sugar, he said in a low, tortured voice: 'I was responsible for the accident, Sally. It—it was my fault!'

She put her hand on his arm. He was trembling violently.

'You're upset, Trevor. Everything is too much for you just now. I should drink this coffee—'

But he shook his head and looked at her, his eyes were bitter.

'I was beside myself with jealousy, Sally,' he muttered. 'Colin's stolen Helen from me. When I knew she was going back to London with him I felt I'd do anything to prevent it. I took my car down the drive before they left, knowing it would be easy to stage an accident. Well, it was easier than I expected.'

She did not know what to say. Fortunately, for him, things had not turned out as tragically as they might have done. Colin was little the worse for the incident and Helen had escaped with hardly a scratch.

'I must go to the police,' Trevor

muttered, crossing to the window and staring blindly out at the garden.

Sally suddenly made up her mind. In a way Colin and Helen deserved all that had happened to them. Trevor had acted unwisely, even wickedly, there could be no doubt about that, but it was not going to help things any to have everything brought up in court and Trevor probably have to go to prison.

She went to his side and said quietly: 'I think I should keep quiet about your part in this affair, Trevor. It won't do any good to wash all this dirty linen in public.'

He turned a haggard face towards her. 'But Helen's guessed—!'

'She can't prove anything. What I should do if I were you, Trevor, is wait for some time until Colin is better and Helen's simmered down a bit. Then you can go to them both and make a clean breast of it. If they want to proceed against you then—well, that will be their business, but I have a feeling they'll want to forget the whole thing.'

A little hope came into his unhappy eyes.

'Do you really think so, Sally?' he muttered.

'I really do. And now drink your coffee. You look as if you need it.'

She gave him the cup and he gulped the hot liquid down eagerly; a little colour came into his cheeks. She turned away to leave the room but he said as she reached the door—'You're a grand girl, Sally. Thank you for—everything.'

Out in the hall she found Alec talking to Dr Bradley and her aunt's companion. 'I've told him he can't possibly go back to London today,' the doctor said. 'He's lucky to have escaped so lightly but he's had a bad shock. In any case he tells me his car's badly damaged and I've suggested that he gets the garage in the village to send someone up to look at it. He and Miss Renton can then take a good rest. They'll probably both be fit to travel to London by train tomorrow.'

'It looks as if we'll have to stay as well, Sally,' Alec put in. 'Our train's gone and there isn't another good one until late this evening.'

'I'd better make the necessary arrangements then,' Martin said with a suspicion of a sniff. Turning, she made off in the direction of the kitchen.

The doctor made up the stairs saying that he might as well see Mrs Pentland and save himself a journey out to Monk's Hollow later. Alec and Sally went back into the sitting-room where Colin, eyes closed, was lying back on the settee with Helen standing a little helplessly by his side. She looked across at the newcomers with relief.

'I've been trying to get him to go to bed,' she said, 'but he doesn't seem to want to move.'

Alec crossed to Colin's side and said firmly: 'Come on now, old chap. You'll be much better once you're in bed. Let me help you!'

Colin, looking up at Alec through half-closed eyes, stayed where he was for a few seconds more, then allowed himself to be helped to his feet. Alec slipped his arm about his waist and drew him towards the door. When they had gone Sally looked at Helen.

'Can I help you, Helen?' she asked. 'You look as if you ought to be lying down. You've gone through a nasty experience.'

But Helen shook her head fiercely. 'I can get to my room under my own steam, thanks,' she said sharply, and walked a little unsteadily out into the hall.

Sally, a little uneasy, watched her go up the stairs and disappear from sight. She was about to go up the stairs after Helen to make quite sure that she had reached her room safely when Dr Bradley appeared and came down the staircase towards her.

'How's my aunt?' she asked eagerly.

Dr Bradley's pleasant face clouded. 'Well, physically, she seems much better,' he said, 'but I can't help feeling there's something on her mind.'

'You think she's worried about something?'

'It's hard to say. She may just be depressed by her accident. After all, she had a very near shave when her bed caught fire.'

'Perhaps it would help if I went in to talk to her,' Sally said. 'In any case I want to tell her that we're all here for another night. I don't suppose she's heard anything about the accident on the drive?'

'No, I didn't tell her. Perhaps it would be as well if you, as her niece, had a little talk to her, Miss Morgan. You must excuse me now. I have a number of other visits to make and I'm late.'

He hurried away and Sally went slowly upstairs. She hesitated outside her great-aunt's room. The old lady would think she was on the way to the station now and that the others were driving towards London.

She tapped on the door, then, when she heard a faint 'Come in!' she turned the handle and went into the room. Mrs Pentland was propped up against her pillows. A book lay in her lap but she was not reading it.

She looked towards Sally and her eyes widened in alarm. 'Sally, what are you doing here? I thought you were—'

Sally went quickly forward. 'Colin collided with Trevor's car on the drive, Aunt Agatha. Nobody's badly hurt but the doctor thinks that Colin shouldn't travel to London today. The accident made Alec and I miss our train and we think we'd better stay overnight again.'

The old lady gave a gasp of dismay. She shook her head, looking at Sally with frightened eyes.

'No, Sally, you mustn't stay here another night,' she said in a trembling voice very unlike her usual vigorous tones. 'You must get a taxi from the village and drive to the junction. It's only a few miles away. Don't heed the expense. I'll pay for the taxi.'

Sally looked at her in astonishment. 'But why shouldn't I stay another night, Aunt Agatha?' she demanded.

The old lady did not reply for several seconds, then, in a voice so low that Sally could hardly catch the words, she said:

'You're not safe at Monk's Hollow any more, Sally. You must go away, do you hear? Tell me you'll do as I say!'

Sally began to say something but at the same moment the door opened and Martin appeared. The woman stood at the bottom of the bed and smiled a little acidly at Sally.

'You mustn't tire your aunt, Miss Morgan,' she said reprovingly. 'The more rest she can get the sooner she is likely to be up and about again.'

'I've just been telling Aunt Agatha that we'll all be staying on another night,' Sally said. 'She doesn't seem to think it's a very good idea.'

Martin frowned as she looked at the old lady. 'Well, it's certain that Mr Brent and

Miss Renton can't leave until tomorrow,' she said, 'and Mr Carley doesn't look too fit, if you ask me. They'd best all better stay another night and leave at the same time.'

Sally, glad of Martin's support, smiled at Aunt Agatha. 'You see, even Martin thinks we ought to stay. Try to get some rest now. I'll look in and see you later today.'

She turned and made for the door again. Before she left the room she glanced back at the bed. But Aunt Agatha had turned her face into the pillow and did not move. By her side her companion stood, hands placidly folded on her middle, looking down at her with a little smile which, for some reason she could not understand, turned Sally's blood cold.

She hurried from the room, wondering why she was suddenly filled with a sense of foreboding.

21

In the Night

That night Sally went to bed early. She had rarely known a day drag on so interminably. Colin, Trevor and Helen had kept to their rooms. Even Alec, as if he was avoiding her, had gone for a long tramp and had not come back until tea time. She believed he was uneasy when he was with her.

He thinks he made a fool of himself when he proposed to me when we were lost in the snow, she thought miserably. I suppose he doesn't want to find himself alone with me again and feel he has to ask me if I've made my mind up one way or the other.

She wondered often, during that day, what she would say if he did ask for an answer. Did she love him? Did she want to go back and live in New Zealand as a farmer's wife?

If only I knew the answer to that

life would be much easier, she thought miserably.

When, at half past seven the gong sounded for dinner, Sally had gone downstairs to find Mr Morris in the hall. The solicitor, who had obviously just arrived, regarded her in astonishment.

'But I thought you'd be back in London by now, Miss Morgan,' he said.

Quickly Sally explained what had happened. 'I didn't expect you'd be returning so soon,' she said. She noticed that he avoided her eyes when he muttered something about having to see her aunt again on business.

He had had dinner with her and Alec. She had been glad of his company. It had saved her from a tête-à-tête with the young New Zealander.

After coffee she had gone to her room. The fire was burning brightly and for some time she sat before it staring into the red embers.

What a strange Christmas it had been. First had come her great-aunt's unexpected invitation, then the news that she and three strangers had an equal chance of inheriting her aunt's money. After that there had been a bewildering sequence of incidents which had ended with her great-aunt telling her and the others that none of them would be mentioned in her will, that the sooner they were out of her house the better.

With a sigh Sally started to undress and get ready for bed. She wondered if she should slip along to Aunt Agatha's room to say good night but she recalled how, earlier that evening, she had tried to see the old lady and how Martin had barred her way into her room, saying that her mistress was not feeling well and could not receive visitors.

I'll go and say good-bye before we leave in the morning, Sally thought as she climbed into bed and turned the light out.

She fell asleep fairly quickly. When she wakened she thought it was early morning for a shaft of bright light was shining through a crack in the curtains, but she soon realised that this was the light of the moon and that it could not be much later than midnight.

She wondered what had wakened her. Had it been some noise which had not been repeated since?

She lay listening and at last her straining

ears picked up a soft thudding noise quite close at hand. She switched on the bedside light and sat up. The noise seemed to have come from behind the dressing-table which stood against the long mirror on the wall.

Her heart gave a sickening lurch. This could only mean that someone was in the secret passage. They must have been trying to open the mirror door and found it blocked by the heavy dressing-table.

Slipping out of bed Sally pulled on a wrap and crossed the room. She looked at the mirror and saw it tremble as if someone was at the other side of it, trying to force it open.

'Who's there?' she called. For a moment there was dead silence. It was as if whoever was at the other side of the mirror was standing there, not knowing whether to make another attempt to enter the room or retreat.

Then, faintly but distinctly, there came to Sally's ear the sound of stealthy footsteps moving away along the passage. Sally stood there, undecided what to do. Every instinct urged her to jump back into bed and pull the sheets over her head, then she knew that she might never get a better opportunity than this to solve the mystery.

She made for the door. If she hurried she could get round through the corridors to the back of the house to the housemaid's cupboard into which the other end of the secret passage led. If she was in time she might then see who had been trying to get into her room for they would be obliged to leave the secret passage by the cupboard as the other exit was blocked.

A little breathless she stood a few yards from the door which led into the cupboard. She noticed that it was slightly ajar, and, with a fast-beating heart, she waited for it to be pushed open and for someone to emerge into the light from the small bulb burning overhead.

But almost a minute passed and no one appeared. Doubts began to grow in her mind. Surely whoever had gone into the secret passage could not still be there. Had they left it before she managed to get round from her bedroom by way of the corridors?

She waited another full minute then went cautiously forward. Pulling the door of the housemaid's cupboard open she looked at the wall beyond which she knew the secret passage lay. It presented a blank vacant face to her.

She did not know what to do. It seemed unlikely that anyone should still be lurking in that pitch-dark passage. The likeliest explanation was that they had left before she had got round to this side of the house.

She went to the foot of the little staircase she and Alec had explored on Christmas Day. She remembered that the door at the top had been locked. She wondered if the person who had been in the secret passage had gone through it a few seconds before.

She stood at the bottom of the steps, one part of her desperately wanting to go back to the safety of her room, the other at the mercy of her curiosity. Finally, she decided that she would go up to the door and satisfy herself that it was still locked. She could then return to her room, having done her best to solve the mystery.

Slowly she mounted the few steps and presently found herself confronted by the door. She put out her hand, found the knob and turned it.

Her heart gave a leap as, instead of

the door resisting her pressure, it opened silently, leaving her free to move forward into the pitch darkness beyond.

She stood there undecided. If only she had had a torch with her. She wondered if there was a light switch beyond the door and took a few tentative steps forward, her hand groping along the wall.

But her fingers encountered nothing but the damp surface. Once more she hesitated. Should she go on or go back?

Suddenly she heard a quick step behind her. She began to turn but she was too late. Something was thrown over her head, something thick which threatened to stifle her. She fought wildly but strong arms were clamped over her own and despair swept over her as she realised that she was helpless.

Suddenly she was thrust violently in the back. She did her best to keep her balance but it was useless. She staggered forward a few steps and tripped over something, then went headlong. She lay, all the remaining breath knocked out of her. She felt to be suffocating and struggled feebly again.

Near at hand she heard a voice say: 'You take that end! I'll take her feet. The sooner we move her the better.'

22

Martin's Story

Sally must have lost consciousness for when she came to someone was standing over her holding a flickering oil lamp. For a moment her mind was a blank. Where was she? What had happened?

'So you've come to, have you?'

It was Mrs Martin's voice. Sally, whose head ached, narrowed her eyes against the light. Suddenly she remembered all that had happened since she had wakened and heard movements in the secret passage.

She tried to speak but no sound came. She realised then that a gag had been placed in her mouth and that her hands were tied behind her back. She tried to get up but a firm hand pressed her down again.

She looked round but all she could see was the light from the lamp flickering on the walls and ceiling and the formidable form towering over her as she lay on the floor.

Panic began to rise in her again. Why was she here? Why had Martin made her a prisoner like this?

Suddenly there came another sound, a stammering gabbling sound. Martin spoke sharply and there was silence again.

'You can get up!'

Sally, meeting the hard eyes in the grim expressionless face, struggled first to her knees, then to her feet. A strong hand closed over her arm and propelled her across the floor to thrust her down on to a hard wooden chair.

'Now, sit there and listen to me,' Martin said in a cold level voice which chilled Sally's blood.

Sally looked round. Strips of old wallpaper hung in tatters from the damp walls. A single bed, the chair on which she sat, a worn rug, a cracked mirror fastened to the stained wall were all the furniture the little room contained. Apparently there was no means of heating the room which was bitterly cold.

'I suppose I should be grateful that you stayed another night at Monk's Hollow,' Martin's voice went on. 'If you'd gone back to London I wouldn't have been able to dispose of you, as I mean to do.'

Sally looked at the other woman, noting the strange gleam in her dark eyes, the way the corners of her mouth twitched.

She's mad, she thought, and a sense of dread came to her heart. What chance would she have against this woman who, in any case, was much stronger than she was. Even if she had not been bound and gagged she would have lost any struggle she might have engaged in with Martin.

Out of the corner of her eye she caught sight of a slight movement across the other side of the room. The oil lamp cast shadows but there was enough light to see a huddled figure crouching on the floor against the wall.

Her heart quickened. So the cowled figure, which she had thought to be a ghost, was this pathetic creature, head bowed as if in shame.

'I suppose you're wondering why I've brought you here,' Martin said in her cold crisp voice.

Sally looked at her, though, because of the gag, she was unable to speak. The woman, dressed in a long robe which apparently concealed her night attire, stood straight as a ramrod, her face grim and relentless.

'I intended you to come and watch the door of the cupboard,' she said with grim satisfaction. 'I was in the secret passage. I purposely made a noise and wakened you. I gambled on your curiosity getting the better of you. I believed you would come hurrying out to watch the door of the cupboard to see who came out.'

When Sally stared at her, unable to speak, Martin glared back at her.

'When you went up the stairs and found the door open I waited until you'd gone into the darkness, then—I came after you. I had a travelling rug with me. I flung it over you and Chrissie helped me to carry you here.'

Sally glanced over to the corner again. The cowled figure at the mention of the name had looked up.

Sally's blood ran cold seeing the hollow eyes, the pale skin. Who was this creature? Martin had called her 'Chrissie'. Yet that meant nothing to her.

She longed to cry out, to demand what Martin wanted with her. But she couldn't speak. The gag had been tied very tightly.

Martin leaned over her. 'You were a fool to come here, Sally Morgan. If you'd stayed away you'd have been safe. But I can't have a chit of a girl stealing the money I've worked for away from me and—and—'

Just for a moment the mad eyes glanced across at the silent cowled figure in the corner. Then they returned to Sally.

'I was only a young woman when I had my child,' the low tortured voice went on, speaking as if to itself. 'The man I married when I was barely old enough to know my own mind deserted me and left me to bring my baby up on my own. I got a succession of jobs, putting my baby out to foster parents. But it was a bitter struggle. However, when Chrissie was old enough to go to school I took the job with your great-aunt. It was good money and I was able to keep Chrissie in comfort.'

She drew a deep breath and began to pace up and down the little room.

'At first all went well. Mrs Pentland liked me and I knew I could just about put up with her bossy ways. The money she paid was good and I decided to be patient for sooner or later, I believed I would get her fortune into my own hands. After all, she was all alone in the world. Chrissie, meanwhile, had left school and got a job. But she was soon in trouble.

It was obvious to me that she was not the same as other girls. She was put on probation, then sent to an approved school, finally to prison.'

Martin's voice had sunk to a whisper so that Sally could hardly hear what she said.

'I never told Mrs Pentland anything of my worries. She thought my husband had died leaving me childless. I thought she might dismiss me if she knew my only child was a—a gaol-bird.'

A sound came from her which was suspiciously like a sob. She went on:

'I took Chrissie to a doctor. They told me she was not—quite normal. They said she ought to be in a—a home for treatment. There was nothing I could do about it. I had to let her go.'

In spite of her predicament Sally felt a wave of pity sweep over her. What a sad story!

Martin stood in front of Sally looking down at her with half-closed eyes.

'Chrissie was in and out of mental homes for a long time. Then—then after she had tried to strangle another patient the authorities said she was not safe to be at large. They told me they were going to put her away for good. I'd never told them where I lived—I wasn't going to have them getting on to Mrs Pentland and spoiling my chances with her. So—so a few weeks ago I brought Chrissie here. She's been here ever since.'

Fascinated, Sally looked at the cowled figure in the corner, now rocking backwards and forwards as it muttered and mumbled to itself.

Mildred the maid had said she had heard strange noises overhead in the night. This explained it. This mad woman, Martin's daughter, had been living up in the attics of Monk's Hollow for weeks. It must have been her movements that Mildred had heard!

She longed to ask her great-aunt's companion what she meant to do with her. But silence was enforced on her by the gag which was almost suffocating her.

'Occasionally Chrissie got out of her quarters,' Martin went on. 'She took to roaming the house and I think she scared some of the servants. They began to think the house was haunted. Briggs said he met her along one of the passages one night and ran back to the kitchen for safety. The silly old fool!'

Martin resumed her pacing up and down the room. She went on in a low monotonous voice:

'When Mrs Pentland fell ill just over two years ago I nursed her back to life. She was very grateful to me. She led me to believe she intended to make a will in my favour. I was happy. When she died I knew I would have enough money to keep Chrissie in my own care, remove for ever the shadow of the public asylum from her life.

'I knew by then, of course, that you, Mrs Pentland's great-niece, were living somewhere in London. She didn't give any hint that she intended to invite you to Monk's Hollow this Christmas. I thought she hated you as much as she had hated your father. I never expected danger from that quarter.'

She stopped in front of Sally who thought she was going to strike her. But a moment later she had resumed her pacing.

'A week before Christmas she told me she had invited five young people down to Monk's Hollow for the holiday and that she intended to make one of them her heir,' Martin said, her voice full of venom. 'I couldn't believe my ears. I was sure she'd made a will in my favour and

240

now it was to be scrapped and another will made in its place.' The voice took on a vicious edge. 'I, it seemed, would just have a legacy to repay me for all my devoted service!'

A fist was shaken in front of Sally's nose.

'But I wasn't going to be done out of the money. I hadn't put up with your great-aunt's bullying for all that time to be fobbed off with a few hundred pounds. No! I wanted the lot—or nothing!'

Sally listened, fascinated. She began to see daylight at last. This explained the visit from the secret passage on her first night, the assault on Helen, the apparition outside the sitting-room window while Colin was telling his ghost story—they had all been a part of the campaign to scare her and the others away from Monk's Hollow so that Aunt Agatha would think them cowards and change her mind about changing her will.

Then when they had refused to be frightened, and the solicitor had come, obviously to change the will, sterner measures had been called for.

As if in answer to her unspoken questions Martin went on:

'I let Chrissie loose once or twice but she didn't manage to scare you away. I even dangled a hood and robe from an upstairs window so that it scared you in the sitting-room on Christmas night. That accounted for there being no footprints in the snow! I realised that more drastic action was needed. I knew that once Mrs Pentland changed her will I'd be lost. So—so I gave her some sleeping pills, and, when she slept, I—I set fire to her mattress. I knew that everyone, including herself, would think, knowing she smoked in bed, that she was responsible. My little plot failed, thanks to you, but no one ever suspected me!'

There was triumph in the mad voice now. Sally tentatively feeling the rope that bound her wrists and despairing of ever getting free, realised that Martin didn't know that her mistress *had* suspected that someone had tried to murder her. The only person she must have spoken to about the attempt on her life must have been her great-niece. She would know that if she told the police they would laugh at her for she had no proof.

Martin's eyes blazed suddenly. 'When I heard my mistress tell you all that she had

242

decided not to alter her will, that she didn't want any of you as her heir, I thought my troubles were over. I knew you'd be away first thing in the morning and that all I need do then was go on nursing the old woman until she died and—and collect!'

She bit her lip. Her voice rose angrily:

'Then what happened. Because of that stupid accident you all came back for another day. And—and Mr Morris returned.'

Sally looked up into the face twisted with hatred. Why was Martin so disturbed that the solicitor had come back? She was soon to know.

'Your aunt had tried to trick me by getting me to think she wasn't changing her will. She might have got away with it too, except that I overheard her talking to Mr Morris this evening. Apparently after she had told you and the others that she wasn't making any of you her heir, she had instructed the solicitor to go to London and draw up a will—in your favour. He came back tonight with it for her signature. I was behind the panelling at the back of your aunt's bed. As you must have suspected, this old house is honeycombed with secret passages. I heard every word that passed.'

Sally could hardly believe her ears. So she was her aunt's heir, after all? But it didn't make sense, not after what Aunt Agatha had said.

Then—remembering how eager the old woman had been for her to leave the house she realised that only one thought had been in Aunt Agatha's mind; her safety now she was committed to having made her her heir.

Martin's face advanced towards her. She could feel the woman's hot breath on her cheek. Her heart sank seeing the mad light in the blazing eyes in the pale twisted face.

'So you see why I can't let you live, Sally Morgan,' the voice said. 'You're your aunt's heir. The new will's been made and signed. If you die I might still come into the money for surely they'd have to accept the old will when your aunt died. And I'll see she doesn't live long now, I can promise you!'

Sally's head swam with horror looking into the mad eyes. Suddenly the walls of the little room in the light of the flickering oil lamp seemed to be closing in on her. She heard a scrambling noise and knew that the cowled figure in the corner had got to its feet and was advancing towards her.

'Come, Chrissie,' Martin's voice muttered, 'you have work to do before daylight.'

Then mercifully she fainted.

23

The Last Act

Alec was wakened by someone tapping lightly on his door. Pulling on his dressing-gown he groped his way, half-asleep, across the room and looked out into the corridor. He was surprised to find Mildred, the maid, her hair in curlers, regarding him with scared eyes.

'What is it?' he asked sharply.

'Please sir, I—I went to Miss Morgan's room,' the girl said tearfully. 'She—she's not there, sir.'

Alec frowned. As far as he could tell it was the middle of the night. What was this girl seeking Sally for at such an hour?

'But—but I don't understand,' he said. 'Why do you want her?'

'It's the noise overhead, sir,' Mildred sobbed. 'I—I told Miss Morgan about it and—and she was interested. It's been going on for some time now, sir, and—and as I was scared I thought I'd come to her and tell her about it. But—she's not there. As you're next door I decided I'd tell you, sir.'

Alec was fully awake now. He nodded approvingly at the girl.

'You did right, Mildred,' he said, 'I'll go along to Miss Morgan's room and see for myself.'

A quick glance at the bedclothes, which had been hurriedly flung back, told him that Sally had left the room some time before. He stood looking uncertainly across at the dressing-table to see if it was still blocking the entrance to the secret passage.

When he found it had not been disturbed he made up his mind. He would go to examine the cupboard into which it led, which he and Sally had found on Christmas Day.

Mildred hurried along behind him.

'What do you think it all means, sir?' she asked anxiously, but he did not reply.

They soon reached the quiet passage. Alec examined the cupboard, but, though the door was slightly ajar, the entrance to the secret passage was sealed. He hesitated. Should he try to enter the secret passage from this end or search for Sally elsewhere? He made a cursory examination of the wall at the back of the cupboard but as he did not immediately see any way of opening it, he turned away.

His eye fell on the flight of steps a little further down the passage. He made for them, Mildred following a few paces behind.

He switched on the torch he had brought with him, and climbed the short staircase to the door at the top. This did not appear to have been opened since he and Sally had examined it on Christmas Day.

He put out his hand to the knob, but before he could grasp it he heard footsteps at the other side of the door. Mildred, just behind him, had heard them too.

'Someone's coming,' she whispered and Alec frowning put his finger to his lips to warn her to keep quiet.

Sally found herself still sitting upright in the wooden chair when she came to. She could not have been unconscious for more than a few seconds.

She looked round. At first she thought she was alone then suddenly she heard the sound of agitated breathing close at hand.

With a great effort she turned her head far enough round to see that someone was sitting by her side regarding her closely.

The woman's cowl had fallen back to reveal sharp features and sly cunning eyes which regarded Sally with a mixture of hatred and fear.

Sally tried to speak but her words were stifled by the gag. She moved, hoping that by some miracle her bonds might have loosened. Then her heart sank with despair realising that she was as helpless as ever.

Thin skeletal hands as cold as ice came out to touch her face and neck. If she had not been gagged she would have screamed. She leaned back as far as she was able, her eyes wide with terror; but the hands followed her and closed about her slender throat.

A muttering came from the thin purple lips as the woman, kneeling before Sally, tightened the grip on her neck.

Sally fought desperately for breath. Now she knew why Martin had left her alone with her daughter. Once before this mad woman had tried to strangle someone, a patient at a mental home where she had been detained.

It only needed Martin to put the idea into her head, perhaps tell the poor creature that Sally was a danger to them both. Later Martin would undoubtedly return, remove the gag and untie her wrists, then leave her to be found. Everybody would believe that she had found her own way into this attic, probably trying to trace the cause of some mysterious noise she had heard, and that she had been set upon by this mad woman who had strangled her...

It was so simple—yet so fiendishly clever... For the worst that could happen to Chrissie Martin would be that she would be sent to a criminal lunatic asylum where she would have gone in any case, for her mother must know that she could not keep her indefinitely at Monk's Hollow.

Stars were dancing before Sally's eyes as she struggled for breath. Once as she kicked desperately at the other woman her foot reached its target. She heard a grunt of pain and the fingers about her throat slackened for a moment. But she had time only to draw in a breath before they tightened on her windpipe again.

The room began to spin before her eyes. The sound as of a torrent roared in her ears. She knew that this was the end. In a few seconds now she would be dead...

Dimly she realised that the hands had been pulled away from her throat, that someone was holding her close. She struggled for breath and felt the life-giving air surge into her labouring lungs.

'Sally! Sally, darling!'

Miracle on miracle, it was Alec's voice.

She clung to him, unable to speak, just content to lie in his arms as slowly the horror receded as overwhelming relief took its place.

An hour later, when the doctor had been and gone, Sally lay in bed, holding Alec's hand as he sat by her side. A bandage was about her bruised throat and she still found it very painful to swallow or talk. But otherwise she felt little the worse for her terrifying experience.

'Martin's as mad as her daughter, of course,' Alec said, 'only in a different way.

It must run in the family. Only a mad woman would try to put such a fiendish scheme into operation. She must have known she could not keep her daughter by her indefinitely and decided to use her in her bid to get your aunt's money before the authorities took her away.'

'I—I suppose she was desperate,' Sally whispered. 'My coming here and her disappointment when my aunt named me as her heir must have been all that was needed finally to turn her brain.'

'Thank God I got to you in time,' Alec muttered. 'If it hadn't been for Mildred—'

'Where's Martin now?'

'They've taken her away. When she pushed past me on the stairs she tried to hide in the secret passage, but they soon fetched her out. They've taken her mad daughter away as well.'

'Poor things, I can't help but feel sorry for them.'

'Sorry! Don't you realise that they tried to murder you?'

She smiled, and, lifting his hand, laid it against her cheek.

'If it hadn't been for them I might never have realised I loved you—until I was back

251

in London and you'd returned to New Zealand,' she murmured. 'Then—then it would have been too late and I'd have spent the rest of my life in bitter regrets.'

He bent to kiss her. 'And now you'll be going back to New Zealand with me. You'll like it, Sally. It's a wonderful country.'

Her eyes shone as she snuggled down against the pillows.

'What a strange Christmas it's been,' she whispered. 'During three days I've not only become an heiress—I've found a husband as well. All the rest doesn't seem to matter any more.'

Later that day they went along to Aunt Agatha's room. The old lady held out her arms to Sally.

'God bless you, my child,' she said. 'I feel much of what has happened has been my fault. I ought to have guessed about Martin before I did. But she was so efficient I never suspected she was only doing her work because she thought she was going to be my heir. It's true I told her she would benefit under the terms of my will, but I never intended to leave her more than a fairly substantial legacy. I'd made arrangements to leave the bulk of my money to charity. Her vivid imagination must have led her to believe she was to be the sole legatee.

'Though I half-suspected she was at the back of the fire when I nearly lost my life, I would have been laughed at if I'd accused her. So I decided to let her think I didn't suspect anything, let her believe I accepted the story that I'd gone to sleep with a lighted cigarette in my hand. But I told Mr Morris to go back to London and draw up another will, naming you, Sally. I thought you'd be well away from the house when he returned. But—well, you weren't and as a result you nearly—'

Sally held the trembling body close.

'Don't think about it any more, Aunt Agatha,' she said gently. 'All's well that ends well.'

She held out her hand to Alec, her eyes shining.

'We have something to say, Aunt Agatha,' she said, looking back at the old lady. 'We want you to be our first guest in our new home.'

Aunt Agatha regarded them in astonishment.

'What! You want me to travel out to New Zealand!'

Alec grinned. 'It isn't as fearsome a

253

journey as all that. Only a few hours by air.'

A little smile spread across the lined old face.

'It's very kind of you and I gladly accept,' she said, then added: 'But it won't be for six months at least. You must have at least so long to yourselves.'

When they had said good night and were alone again Alec said slipping his arm around Sally's slim waist: 'Your aunt's a sensible old girl. That six months is going to be a wonderful time for me, Sally. Call me selfish if you like, but I've so much to share with you, so much to learn about you. After all, we've only known each other a few days.'

Sally did not speak. What was there to say? A life full of promise stretched before them with not a cloud in the sky.

This Large Print Book for the Partially sighted, who cannot read normal print, is published under the auspices of

THE ULVERSCROFT FOUNDATION